'Where are y‍ **demanded.**

'Home,' Antonia whispered. 'I'm going home. There's nothing left for me here.'

'I'm here,' he murmured gruffly.

'No, you're not.' She shook her head. 'You're standing aloft in a place I can never reach you. It's called the social ladder. You don't mind coming down to the bottom rung to enjoy life with the masses now and then, but when it comes to elevating someone up to your top rung—no chance.' She laughed. It was a bitter sound. 'Elite marries elite. Darling Mamma expects it.'

'Leave my mother out of this,' he rasped back angrily.

'Why should I? In truth, I'm grateful for what your mother did tonight. Because she forced me to take a good look and see just how I had been wasting my life here with you.'

'Wasting it because I haven't asked you to marry me?' he threw back. 'Is that what your year-long investment in me has really been about, *cara*?'

'I invested in *love*!' she cried.

Michelle Reid grew up on the southern edges of Manchester, the youngest in a family of five lively children. But now she lives in the beautiful county of Cheshire with her busy executive husband and two grown-up daughters. She loves reading, the ballet, and playing tennis when she gets the chance. She hates cooking, cleaning, and despises ironing! Sleep she can do without, and produces some of her best written work during the early hours of the morning.

Recent titles by the same author:

THE SPANISH HUSBAND
A SICILIAN SEDUCTION
THE UNFORGETTABLE HUSBAND

THE BELLINI BRIDE

BY
MICHELLE REID

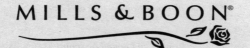

*First published in Great Britain 2001
Harlequin Mills & Boon Limited,
Eton House, 18-24 Paradise Road, Richmond, Surrey TW9 1SR*

© Michelle Reid 2001

ISBN 0 263 82546 9

*Set in Times Roman 10½ on 12 pt.
01-1101-49953*

*Printed and bound in Spain
by Litografía Rosés, S.A., Barcelona*

CHAPTER ONE

THE BED was a sea of rumpled white linen. Tangled amongst it Marco Bellini could see a long golden leg bent at the knee and the smooth silken-curve of a hip and thigh. The rest was covered by fine white sheeting but for a slender arm and the rippling swathe of strawberry-blonde hair flowing away from the kind of profile that would have launched ships in times gone by.

Only her name was not Helen, it was Antonia, and, although her beauty might have launched many metaphorical ships in her time, there was no disputing to whom she now belonged.

Leaning back against the balcony rail, Marco allowed himself a smile as he brought his coffee cup to his lips. It was still very early, but the sun was already hot against his naked back. He had come out onto the terrace directly from his shower, and the white towel draped low around his narrow hips was his only concession to modesty, here, in his summer villa perched high on the hill above Portofino, where the only eyes to see him belonged to the seagulls soaring on the early morning currents of air.

And Antonia, of course, if she bothered to wake up. But, unlike him, she didn't have to be back in Milan by nine o'clock, so she had no reason to rise this early. Although… he then added ruefully to that, if she did happen to awaken now, it would be the simplest thing in the world for him to linger long enough to drop the towel and join her back in the bed.

5

But not yet, Marco told himself as he took another sip from his cup. The coffee was hot, black and strong and was just another pleasure he enjoyed lingering over while he leant here watching his woman sleep.

In the year they had been together he had never seen Antonia look anything but beautiful. Dressed to slay or stripped bare to the exquisite skin nature had given her, she exuded a beauty that by far outclassed any other woman he had known. He was proud to be her lover, proud that only he held the right to place a possessive hand upon any part of her anatomy. Proud that she only had eyes for him.

But did he love her? he asked himself.

No, he admitted heavily. He didn't love her. He loved how she looked, and how she always made him feel. And he would willingly have laid down his own life if it meant him saving hers. But true love had to go deeper than that. He had to love *what* she was, and he didn't.

A sigh caught in the depth of his chest. A cloud blotted out the sun. A seagull shrieked in protest. The coffee suddenly tasted bitter. Putting the cup aside he turned to stare at the misted-blue waters of the Mediterranean shimmering in the distance—and wished to hell he knew what he was going to do about her.

Letting her go was out of the question. Letting her stay meant trouble in more ways than one. Out there, across hills and lush valleys that made up his beautiful Italy, trouble was brewing. It came in the form of an autocratic mother and an ailing father with an urgent desire to see his son safely married and settled before he died.

Marrying Antonia, even without the true-love bit, would be the easiest thing in the world for him to do. She was young, she was beautiful and she loved him totally. But what parent would condone their only son, and the heir to the great Bellini fortune, marrying himself to a woman like Antonia?

A woman with the kind of past that was destined to dog her for ever. A woman with the kind of past that would reflect poorly on him *and* his family name.

A woman who made the perfect mistress—but could never be the perfect wife for him.

Another sigh whispered from him. Maybe Antonia heard it, because she began to stir. Recovering his coffee-cup, Marco turned to watch her slide lazily onto her back then, even before she bothered to open her eyes, send an arm out to search the empty space beside her in the bed. It was a gesture so familiar to him that he actually felt the hairs on his chest prickle as if she had reached out and touched him. The sensation placed the smile back on his lips, because it pleased him to know that the first thing she always thought about on waking was him.

When she found no warm male body lying beside her, her next move was to open her lovely eyes, pause for a moment to allow the remnants of sleep to disperse, then, in a single smooth graceful movement, she sat up and began to search for him.

She found him almost instantly. A warm lover's smile touched her lovely mouth. '*Ciao*,' she greeted him softly.

His response was a lazy masculine gleam over the rim of his cup, while inside he became aware of the chemical responses already beginning to stir his blood. She moved him in so many ways he didn't dare count them.

Sliding out of the bed, she lifted her arms above her head and indulged in a long lazy stretch that highlighted every perfect contour of her very naked frame from slender toes to delicate fingertips. Her light golden skin shone like the finest silk ever created. Her wonderful hair tumbled in loosely spiralling threads down her arching spine. In all his life Marco had never known any woman quite so perfect as Antonia. Her face, her hair, her sensational body—the way she moved as she began to walk towards him.

Like the world's most dangerous siren, she roused the male senses without even having to try. Even the sun worshipped her by coming out from behind its cloud at the same moment she stepped onto the terrace, pooling her in soft golden light as she continued her slow graceful journey towards him.

It was no wonder Stefan Kranst had been so obsessed with her, Marco thought with a sudden grimness. No wonder he'd painted her every single way an artist could paint an obsession. Seeing her like this, he could easily understand why the man had felt so compelled to preserve her naked image. For years Antonia had appeared in all of his paintings, not always the main focal point but always the slender naked figure you looked for whenever you found yourself viewing a Kranst.

But in his desire to make Antonia immortal he had turned her into every man's titillating fantasy. Her naked form now adorned the walls of the rich and famous. When she walked into a room those in the know stopped and stared in intimate recognition.

Did she care? No. Did she blush with embarrassment or hide her eyes in shame? Not this woman, who was as comfortable with her body as she was comfortable with those wretched paintings.

As for him? Marco was very much aware that Antonia's notoriety as Stefan Kranst's famous nude model gave him a certain kudos amongst his envious peers. But it didn't mean he liked it, only that he had learnt to accept it because, like Kranst in a way, he was obsessed with the woman—though not the haunted creature held captive in oils.

Coming to a halt directly in front of him, Antonia said absolutely nothing but just held his gaze as she folded slender white fingers over the strong brown ones he had wrapped around his coffee cup. Her eyes gleamed like topaz in the sun, his darkened into humour as she guided the cup towards her own mouth and took a few delicate sips at the coffee before just as silently lifting the cup to his own mouth.

More than happy to play this little game the way she wanted him to play it, Marco obediently drank while their eyes remained locked in the beginnings of seduction. With both mouths moistened by warm black coffee, she then guided the cup away, lifted herself up on bare tiptoes, and replaced it with a kiss.

The aroma of coffee swirled all around them, its erotic taste flavoured their mouths, the points of her breasts hovered a soft-breath away from his chest and, beneath the towel, his body began to respond.

This was making love on a different level, this was intimacy so deep it touched parts of him never otherwise touched.

As she drew away again, her eyes held a promise. Maybe he would take her up on it in a minute, Marco idly considered. But for now he was content to enjoy the more simple pleasure of being the passive one while she did the seducing.

She began it by touching a finger to the satin tight hollow of his shoulder. 'You showered without me,' she complained.

He smiled a lazy smile. 'You were asleep,' he reminded her.

She was not in the least bit impressed by that answer, and her mouth took on a sulky pout. Taking the coffee-cup from his fingers she put it aside, took possession of both his hands and fed them round her slender waist, then lifted her own up to curve his nape. One small step and she was fitting her hips into the cradle of his hips and pressing her wonderful breasts against him. Then her head tilted back a little, her sulky mouth parted—and claimed his with another kiss designed to devour.

He would have to be made of stone not to respond to her. He would have to be half the man he actually was not to want what was being offered to him. It was special. *She* was special. He didn't want to lose it.

'What was that for?' she broke the kiss to demand when she felt him shiver.

'The sun has gone in again,' he said.

And it had, he noticed. Like a bad omen, it had slid behind another cloud the moment he'd begun thinking about the future.

'Big softy,' she chided, her fingers tangling lovingly into his hair. 'You want to try standing like this on an English balcony. You would die of frostbite, being such a thin-blooded Italian.'

He was supposed to laugh or come back with a light counter-charge, Marco was well aware of that. But he could do neither because he was suddenly seeing *her* standing naked on that English balcony.

Seeing her exactly as she had once been caught for posterity in a Kranst painting.

'You would know, of course,' was therefore the cynical taunt that slid from him.

Her sudden stillness was electric. If he'd slapped her

he couldn't have achieved a better response. Kiss-warmed lips lost all of their softness. Warm topaz became cold grey glass. With a single step she completely separated herself from him and, without a single word, she turned and walked back into the bedroom.

Remorse played havoc with his conscience as he watched her sensual stride take her towards the bathroom. The urge to go after her and apologise came a couple of short seconds too late. The door closed, he heard the bolt slide home and knew he now had one hell of a task on his hands to put right the wrong he had just done.

'*Damn,*' he cursed as he spun away.

The sun crept out from behind its cloud again. He scowled at it. Scowled at the seagull soaring overhead. Then he scowled at himself because he knew that putting right a wrong would not solve the dilemma that was sitting right on his doorstep waiting to be addressed.

On the other side of the bathroom door, Antonia stood with her eyes closed, waiting for the hurt contracting the muscles around her heart to ease. It hadn't been the words but the way he had said them, with derision, deliberately aimed to cut.

Stefan, she thought wearily. It always came back to Stefan, and Marco's inability to accept the life she had led before she met him. For a man who prided himself on his fast-track modern sophistication, he harboured some truly archaic principles.

One of these days she would find the strength to stand firm and challenge those principles, and this right he felt he had to speak to her like that, she promised herself.

But not yet, she conceded heavily. She just didn't have that kind of strength yet. Because to challenge him meant challenging their whole relationship, and the day she did that Antonia knew would be the same day she lost Marco for good.

Though that moment was coming closer, she recognised, as the hurt began to fade much sooner than it usually did after one of his well-aimed barbs. And she found she could open her eyes and actually look at herself in the mirror opposite without wincing at what she saw.

And what did she see?

She saw a scarlet woman, she grimly mocked that reflection. A woman who was a mistress to a man who wasn't even married but who still classed her as a mistress not a lover. In her view, there was a very important difference between the two titles. To be a man's lover carried a certain amount of moral equality. To be his mistress showed a distinct lack of moral value. And was there such thing as a master to level out the playing field? No, of course not. He remained simply the lover, with no stigma at all attached to the title. You could have a pair of lovers but you could not have a pair of mistresses—not in this context anyway. No, that unenviable title belonged exclusively to her own fair sex.

Sex being the operative word here. She lived in his home, she slept in his bed, and she relied on his financial generosity for her day-to-day survival. In return she gave him her absolute loyalty and her body—the true definition of a mistress, in other words.

Not a bad life for a girl who came from nothing, she supposed. In fact, it would be pretty much a perfect life—if she didn't love him as desperately as she did. Loving Marco made it a miserable life.

How had Stefan described Marco when he'd tried to talk her out of coming to Italy to live with him? 'He's one of life's élite,' he'd said. 'He might want your body, but he will never want you the way you want him to want you. You're not of the fellowship, my darling. It is a simple fact of life that élite marries élite.'

Tough but wise words, as she'd found out the hard way. And if she had any sense at all she would get out, she told her reflection. She would gather up what little bit of pride she had left, and go, before he cleaned her out completely.

And maybe she would do—soon, she resolved.

But she turned away from the mirror as she thought it, knowing that it would take more than the occasional cruel remark on his part to make her leave him. She loved him too much and had stuck with him too long to give up so easily.

Which didn't mean she was going to forgive him, she determined as she stepped into the shower cubicle. Forgiveness came at a price, and Marco was going to have to pay that price with some serious grovelling.

A smile touched her mouth, the very idea of making the arrogant Marco Bellini grovel doing wonders for her mood.

He was gone from the bedroom by the time she reappeared. Gone from the villa too, she discovered when she came downstairs to find Nina, the maid, clearing away what looked like a hastily eaten breakfast.

'Signor Bellini left for Milan ten minutes ago, *signorina*,' she informed her. 'He said to remind you about the party tonight and to tell you to drive carefully, for the summer traffic between here and Milan is reputed to be very bad.'

Antonia thanked the maid for the message, and

smiled in recognition of the routine. Marco was making himself scarce because he knew he had hurt her, but making sure he kept the lines of communication open as he went.

Why? Because for a big tough corporate leader, with a reputed heart of stone and a tongue of steel, when it came to her, he hated dissension. He might not love her the way she wanted to be loved, but he loved her enough to feel uncomfortable when he had upset her. And, being a very selfish man, Marco liked to be comfortable in his private life.

Hence the message telling her to drive carefully, and the reminder about the party tonight. This was Marco putting down the first stepping-stones back to his precious comfort. Other stepping-stones would follow at timely intervals, Antonia predicted as she sat down to eat breakfast, alone for the first time in the week they had just spent here doing very little but making love and sleeping.

A week he'd arranged as a surprise treat for her birthday—along with the natty red Lotus which now stood in the courtyard waiting for her to drive it back to Milan. Last year he had given her a sweet little Fiat to use to get around in. But she had only been with him for a month then, so the value of the gift had reflected that.

Like a bonus for time put in, she likened, and wondered what he would think a fitting bonus for her next birthday.

If she was still around, she added, felt her heart give a tug, and got up from the table to go back upstairs to pack, refusing to answer that little sarcasm—or question why her heart had given that singular tug.

An hour later, dressed in a pair of slender white Capri

pants and a skimpy-red T-shirt, her hair stylishly contained on the top of her head, Antonia was sitting in the creamy interior of the red Lotus, reading the note Marco had left for her on the dashboard.

'Respect the car's power and it will respect you,' it said. 'I prefer you to arrive home to me in one beautiful piece.'

Antonia's smile held a hint of softness this time—not at the message itself so much as the way that Marco had taken time to pause long enough to sit here and write this before climbing into his Ferrari and driving away.

It was another stepping-stone neatly laid, and she was still smiling when she put her new toy into gear, then began following his long journey back to Milan, idly pondering on what his next move would be.

He was nothing if not a brilliant tactician. He waited until she'd reached the outskirts of Milan before making contact again.

Then her mobile began to ring.

Glancing down to where it sat in its hands-free housing, Antonia pondered for a few rings whether to ignore it and just let him stew. But, in the end, irresistible temptation won over stubbornness and, with a flick of a button, she sanctioned the connection.

'*Ciao, mi amore.*' The deep dark tones of his voice filled the car-space, soft, warm and aimed to seduce, she felt tingles of excitement run down her spine. 'You were, of course, too busy concentrating on your driving to answer the phone straight away.'

Not a question exactly, but more a remark loaded with satire. He knew she had hesitated over whether to speak to him.

'What do you want?' she demanded curtly.

'That depends,' he murmured suggestively, 'on where you are right now...'

'Walking naked down Monte Napoleon, living up to expectations,' she promptly tossed back at him, naming a particularly classy area within Milan's famous Quadrilatero.

As a direct hit back at what he had said to her this morning, it should have caught him on the raw. Instead, it was the turn of his appreciative laughter to coil itself all around her. Antonia wriggled in her seat and wished she could hate him. But what she was experiencing was far from hate, and it took a couple of risky manoeuvres through the heavy traffic to help dispel the sensation.

'And to think,' he said eventually, 'I refused lunch at Dino's just to talk to you.'

'Bad move, *caro*,' Antonia responded. 'Dino's was by far your better option.'

'And you sulk like a prima donna,' he smoothly threw back.

He was right and she did. But then she felt justified. Still, the remark held a warning she would be a fool not to heed. 'You told me you had back-to-back meetings all day,' she murmured with less sarcasm. 'Lunch at Dino's is usually an all-afternoon thing.'

'I surprise myself sometimes with my own efficiency,' was his light reply.

'And your conceit,' she added.

'*Si*, that too,' he had the arrogance to agree.

Despite not wanting it to, Antonia felt her mouth twitch into a grin. In truth, his arrogance and conceit were major parts of what made Marco the charismatic person he was. Plus his sensational dark good looks, she then wryly added as she sped off the *autostrada* and headed for the city centre. Then there was his great body, and his prowess as lover, and the way he...

'In truth, lunch at Dino's was never an option.' The sound of his voice grabbed her attention back again. 'The morning meetings ran overtime. The first one of the afternoon begins in half an hour. So here I am, sitting at my desk, with a take-away sandwich to ease my hunger, a newspaper to feed my mind—and a desperate desire to hear you say something nice to me.'

'Huh,' was all she offered.

'You really want me to grovel, don't you?' his rueful voice drawled.

'Preferably on your knees,' Antonia confirmed.

'Mmm,' Marco murmured. 'Now this sounds interesting. There are so many—many ways I can beg your forgiveness from that position.'

Her impulsive burst of laughter refused to be held in check. Across the city haze, in his plush office, Marco leant back in his chair and smiled a satisfied smile. Then, with the charm of a master, he turned the conversation to more ordinary things, like the performance of the Lotus, what she intended to do with her afternoon, and what time they needed to leave the apartment this evening to attend the first wedding anniversary party being thrown by his best friend Franco and his lovely wife Nicola.

By the time he replaced the receiver, Marco was satisfyingly sure that this morning's stupidity on his part had been carefully soothed away and he could begin to relax again.

Reaching out, he picked up his sandwich and removed it from its wrapping, then collected up his newspaper, he lifted his feet onto the corner of the desk, and settled back to enjoy a half-hour of leisure before his next meeting began with a pair of young hopefuls who wanted his financial backing for their very good idea but fell short of his investment criteria by possessing the business skills of a pair of gnats!

Until five minutes ago he had been intending to send them away with the curt advice to learn how to run a business before attempting to start one. But now he felt much more amenable. Maybe he would even offer to oversee the project himself!

Then he opened the newspaper and any hint of amenability died a death in that moment. For there staring out at him was none other than—Stefan Kranst. He was standing inside one of Milan's most respected private art galleries. And the full-page article was really a plug for the Romano Gallery, where the artist was planning to exhibit next week.

But that wasn't the thing that was knotting up Marco. It was the unsavoury suspicion that if Kranst was in town then Antonia must know about it, but she hadn't mentioned a word to him!

Did she know?

Was she planning to meet up with him secretly? She had done it before at least once, to his knowledge.

Antonia might have left Kranst to come to live in Milan with him, but the ex-lovers had not parted enemies. During a trip to London earlier this year, he had discovered by pure accident that she had spent a whole day with Kranst.

'Don't tell me who I can and who I can't see!' she'd declared when he'd objected. 'Stefan will always be very special to me, and if you can't cope with that, then that's your problem, not mine, Marco.'

It had been one of a very few times when she'd actually looked ready to walk away from him if he tried to push the issue. He hadn't pushed it. But, for the first time in his life, he'd experienced the ugly burn of jealousy, when he'd realised that Kranst held a power over Antonia that was a challenge to his own.

He didn't like it. He didn't like the knowledge that he'd backed down from taking up that challenge. And he didn't like Kranst turning up in Milan just when Marco was having to do some serious thinking about his relationship with Antonia.

It was either immaculate timing on Kranst's part or yet another bad omen. Either way, the sandwich never got eaten and the two young hopefuls lost all chance of meeting an amiable Marco Bellini that day. If it hadn't been for the fact that Marco was still functioning clearly enough to recognise an unmissable opportunity in what they were proposing, he would have taken great delight in kicking them out!

Irritation alternated with disturbing bouts of skin-prickling restlessness throughout the rest of the afternoon. Sudden flashes of Antonia and Kranst holed-up somewhere secret played games with his head.

In the end he could stand it no longer and went back to the privacy of his office to pick up the phone. Her mobile was switched off. Irritation ripped through him, then he remembered her telling him she was going straight back to the apartment, so he rang there instead.

All he got was his own pre-recorded message telling him that no one was available to take his call.

Antonia was standing in a tiny backstreet in another, less fashionable part of the city, fitting a key into a door. Once inside, she walked the narrow hallway and began climbing bare-boarded flights of stairs, passing by small dingy offices belonging to the kinds of businesses

Marco looked down upon from his lofty position at the top of the corporate tree. Some of the tenants knew her, some didn't, most looked curiously at her, smiled politely and left her alone. She liked it that way. For this place was her secret. A part of her life Marco didn't control.

On the very top landing, she went to the only door there and fitted another key into its lock. Stepping inside, she carefully closed the door again and then, turning round, she looked about her and quite simply smiled…

CHAPTER TWO

WALKING through the front door to the Milan apartment was always a pleasure. And the first thing Antonia did as she stepped into it some hours later was pause for a moment to reacquaint herself with surroundings that were a thousand times different from those she had just come from.

Occupying the entire top floor of a modern city block, Marco's home was an interior designer's idea of heaven. No detail had been skimped in an effort to achieve its harmonious ambience.

The hall was large and light and airy, the rooms leading off from it furnished with a clever mix of classical, old and new. Nothing offended the eye. There were formal rooms used only for entertaining, less grand rooms for when they did not. The kitchen was a cook's paradise, all four *en-suite* bedrooms designed to co-ordinate with the pastel colours applied to the walls. And everywhere you went you walked on the very best in Italian ceramic, passing between priceless works of art that adorned the walls.

Like his famous art-collecting ancestors, Marco had inherited an eye for what was just that bit special. Both he and his mother were generous patrons of the arts. What either of them bought, others took particular notice of. And, as with his taste in décor, he thought nothing of mixing the totally unknown with old respected masters—and of course it had worked beautifully.

But she didn't have time to stand here considering

all of this right now, Antonia told herself wryly. She was late and she knew it. Somehow, time seemed to have got away from her today, and she was aware that she'd only just made it back before Marco usually arrived home.

Live dangerously, why don't you? she scolded herself as she headed directly for the bedroom, meaning to make it look as if she had been in there for ages getting ready for the evening when he did eventually get in.

It turned out to be a wasted effort for, as fate would have it, Marco didn't appear until she was already dressed for the evening and beginning to wonder what had happened to him.

Then the bedroom door suddenly swung open and he came striding in.

'You're late,' she immediately chided.

'I have a watch,' he clipped back, and walked right past her without even sparing her a glance.

Frowning slightly, Antonia watched him begin pulling off his jacket in a way that spoke volumes about his mood.

'Bad day?' she quizzed.

'Bad everything,' he said grimly.

'Hence no welcoming smile for me, no kiss hello?' Teasing though her voice sounded, she was serious. After the efforts he'd put in, sweet-talking himself back into her favour, this new attitude was threatening to send him right back to square one if he wasn't careful.

Maybe he realised it because, after tossing the jacket onto the bed, he then stood for a moment flexing his wide shoulders as if he was trying to dislodge whatever it was that was bugging him. As she watched solid muscle move beneath pale blue shirting, Antonia felt the usual sprinkling of pleasure warm her insides, and would have gone to him and helped ease those tense muscles—if he hadn't released a sigh and turned to look at her.

The expression on his face held her stationary. His eyes were glinting with barely suppressed anger, his features hard and grim and unusually pale. In a single brief sweep he gave her appearance the once-over, then his mouth tightened and he turned away again.

Warning bells began to ring in her head. 'What's wrong?' she asked sharply.

'Nothing,' he clipped out. Then on another short sigh added, 'Give me ten minutes to make myself human and we will begin this conversation again, I think.'

'Fair enough,' she agreed. It wasn't often she'd witnessed the darker side of Marco, but on those few occasions she had done so, she'd learned very quickly to tread warily around him until he had calmed down. But she was still frowning as she let herself out of the bedroom, wondering what could have happened this afternoon to put him in that kind of mood.

Bad meeting? A fortune lost on the Stock Exchange? she mused as she walked into the small sitting room and straight over to the drinks bar to mix him his favourite whisky sour while she waited for him to join her.

The ten minutes he'd allocated himself had obviously not been long enough, was her first observation when he joined her. He came into the room with his hair still slightly damp from his quick shower and his fingers impatiently tugging the white cuffs to his shirt into line with the black silk edges of his dinner jacket—and it was clear, by the look on his face, that he was feeling no better.

'Here, try this. It might help,' she drily suggested, offering him the prepared drink.

But, 'No time,' he refused. 'And anyway, I'm driving.' With that, he diverted over to the mirror and began messing with his bow-tie.

And the hand holding out the whisky sour sank slowly back to the drinks bar as it began to dawn on Antonia that his mood had nothing to do with a bad day at the office, but had something to do with her.

'All right,' she said, deciding to take him on so they could get whatever it was that was annoying him out of the way before the evening began. 'Tell me what it is I'm supposed to have done to make you so angry.'

'Who said you'd done anything?' Bow-tie perfect, shirt-cuffs straight, he turned his attention to checking his watch. 'If you're ready, we should get going…'

If she was ready… Dipping her eyes to look down at the slender red silk dress she was wearing—newly bought this afternoon with Marco in mind because he loved to see her in red—Antonia felt her own happy mood shatter. The dress, the way she'd done up her hair so only the odd fine silk tendril caressed her nape, and even the blush-red lipstick she was wearing, had all been chosen with his pleasure in mind.

And it hurt that he was deliberately ignoring that. That his voice might sound mellow but the message was cold. Cold like the silence he was now allowing to develop, even when he must know what she was thinking because he deciphered atmospheres in a room as easily as he deciphered a page full of figures.

The man was an accounting genius, it therefore went without saying that he wanted her to feel this hurt. But more painful was the knowledge that he had done this to her twice in one day.

What was the matter with him? What was he trying to tell her with these violent swings in his mood?

That he'd had enough? That she'd begun to irritate him so much that he couldn't seem to look at her without taking a verbal swipe at her?

The idea wasn't a new one. She had been suspecting it on and off for a while, though until this morning they had just enjoyed a whole week of near perfect harmony and she had begun to believe that she'd been imagining his growing irritation with her.

But now, as she stood here in this carefully orchestrated silence, the suspicion returned with a vengeance. Was she growing stale? Did he want out? Had the week away been arranged in an effort to recapture what he was no longer feeling for her?

Twice in one day, she repeated to herself. Twice he'd been deliberately hurtful.

'Cara?' he prompted her to answer.

The endearment made her insides wince. 'Yes,' she said quietly. 'I'm ready.'

But, as she turned away to retrieve her little red purse from where she had left it, she found herself wondering exactly what it was she was ready for. Losing him?

A sharp pain caught her breath for a moment, holding her still while she waited for it to ease in much the same way she had done this morning. By that example the sensation should have dispersed quickly. But it didn't. In fact, the more sure she became that he was tiring of her, the more it was beginning to hurt. Yet she had always known that this could only ever be a temporary affair, she tried to reason. And, as some people were always eager to tell her, she had lasted longer than most.

Those were usually the same people who were also quick to explain that when Marco Bellini married it would be to a woman of his own social standing. Someone with money, someone with class, someone with a lineage to match the superior weight of his. And, most importantly, someone his parents would welcome with open arms.

Certainly not a little English nobody who had never known her father. A woman who wasn't deemed fit to even be in the same room as any of his relatives. And, worse, a woman who didn't mind exposing her body to the world.

'What's this?' The questioning sound of Marco's voice impinged on her bleak summing up of herself. Having to blink a couple of times before she could face him, she found him standing there with a gold-wrapped flat package in his hands.

'Oh, it's a gift for Franco and Nicola.' Eyes still slightly glazed, she turned away again. 'I realised we hadn't got them anything, so I went shopping before coming on here…'

Shopping.

For several moments Marco couldn't move a single muscle. Remorse was cutting into him for the second time that day. While he'd been suspecting her of meeting secretly with Stefan Kranst she'd been trawling the shops, looking for an anniversary gift for his own two closest friends.

He didn't know what to do. He didn't know what to say to put right the wrong he'd done her—yet again. 'I'm sorry, *cara*,' seemed the only thing to offer. 'I should have thought about this myself.'

There was a double meaning to the last part, though he was relieved Antonia couldn't know it. She winced at the *cara*, though, he noticed. Shrugged at the rest. 'It doesn't matter. Your money paid for it.'

With that she walked stiffly away, leaving her very derisive offering hanging in the air behind her. With a silent curse aimed at his own nasty suspicions, Marco followed, grimly deciding to keep his mouth shut since he was well aware that he had successfully managed to wipe her clean of all hint of good humour by now.

And she looked gorgeous, delectable, good enough to eat—though he knew he had left it too late to tell her that. The dress was short, red and very sexy the way it clung to every slender curve she possessed. It made him want to run his hands all over her, but that was just another pleasure he had denied himself with his lousy mood.

Antonia lifted the latch on the front door and stepped through, leaving Marco to set the alarm and lock up, while she called the lift. It arrived as he did. They stepped inside it. The lift took them down towards the basement with Antonia occupying one corner, he another, and the atmosphere was so thick he could have cut it with a knife.

If the English were brilliant at only one thing, then it would have to be their ability to freeze people out, he mused as he viewed her glacial expression.

'Do you want me to apologise for taking my bad temper out on you?' he sighed eventually.

'What—again?' she drawled. Then, 'No, don't bother,' she advised, before he could answer. 'No doubt you'll be doing it again before too long, which renders your apologies pretty meaningless gestures.'

Perhaps he deserved that, Marco conceded. But irritation began to bite into him again. He didn't like being treated like a leper just because he'd made a natural mistake.

Natural? He quizzed himself.

Yes, damn natural, he insisted arrogantly. He might no longer suspect her of spending the afternoon with Kranst, but that didn't mean she didn't *know* the man was here in Milan!

Well, he was damned if he was going to bring the subject up first, he decided, grimly aware that he didn't really want to know the answer. For to know the answer meant dealing with it. And he didn't want to deal with anything that could risk his relationship with Antonia. Not until he had made up his own mind where it was going to go, anyway.

So, with that niggling little confession to chew on, he let the atmosphere remain thick for the next thirty seconds it took the lift to sink. They left it side by side, to walk between the rows of parked cars towards his Ferrari, passing by her neatly parked red Lotus without either of them sparing it a glance.

Three days old and she doesn't even see it. Which, in its own way, made the car just another wasted gesture on his part, he noted testily. She had been ecstatic when he took her away for a week as part of her birthday present, but the car had produced only the usual polite remarks people use when they're given something they're really not that impressed with.

With ingrained good manners that went back a lifetime, he opened the passenger door of the Ferrari and remained standing by it while Antonia slipped gracefully inside. For the briefest of moments only a few centimetres separated them. It was the closest they'd been since this morning on the balcony in Portofino, he realised, as her delicate perfume filled his nostrils and his senses reacted in their usual way.

Grimly, he ignored their message, when only yesterday he would have been freely indulging every sense he possessed.

With his lips pressed together in a steadily darkening mood of discontent, he placed the gift for Franco and Nicola on her lap, closed the door, then rounded the car bonnet to get in beside her. As he settled himself into his seat he caught a glimpse of her icy profile, clenched his teeth together, and turned his attention to getting them moving.

And the silence between them was still so bad it murdered normal body functions like breathing and swallowing. He couldn't stand it. 'Are you going to tell me what's in the parcel?' he asked as lightly as he could in the circumstances.

'A painting,' she answered briefly.

Having already worked that part out for himself, by the shape and the feel of the gift, Marco took a deep breath for patience. 'What kind of painting?' he prompted.

'Why?' she flicked back. 'Are you worried that I don't have the right credentials to choose something acceptable for your friends?'

At which point he gave up. In this kind of mood she was impossible. Sinking back into stiff silence, neither spoke again for the rest of the journey.

Franco and Nicola de Maggio lived in a large house in one of the select residential areas out on the edges of the city. Arriving so late meant it was difficult to find a parking space in the long driveway. Cursing beneath his breath, Marco had to do some pretty deft manoeuvring to slot the long car in between two others already parked. By the time he switched off the engine the atmosphere between them was so tight you could have played an overture on its taut threads.

It was no wonder Antonia was eager to escape from it.

Marco released a hard sigh as he watched her fumble in her rush to unlock her seat belt. 'The filthy atmosphere remains here in the car,' he bit out warningly. They were about to go amongst *his* friends, after all. He had no wish for them to witness his less than harmonious love life.

The false smile she turned on him set a nerve ticking in his jaw—and had other parts of him rising to its provocative bait. He could soften her in seconds, right here, in these cramped confines. He knew a few simple moves that would remind her as to *why* she was even sitting here at all!

'Get out of the car,' he growled at her before he replaced the thought with a very satisfying action.

Antonia didn't need telling for she was already opening the door. Stepping out of air-conditioned coolness into the heat of an Italian summer evening, she stood there taking in a few deep breaths of that air in the vague hopes that it would help warm her up inside.

No chance. Now the suspicion that he was growing weary of her had set itself as cold hard fact in her head, the idea of feeling warm ever again was impossible to imagine.

In truth, she had almost refused to come tonight. For a few minutes, back there in the apartment, she had almost taken the mammoth step of taking the initiative and calling it a day. She had her pride after all. And *it* had no wish to cling on to something that was already dying, even if Marco was willing to hang on until the whole affair had finally strangled itself to death.

But then he'd brought her attention to the gift for Franco and Nicola and she'd changed her mind. The couple might be Marco's friends, but they had also become *her* friends over the last year—Nicola especially. Leaving Marco was one thing. Doing it on the night of Nicola's wedding anniversary party would cast a black cloud over her friend's special night, and she had no wish to do that.

And anyway, she admitted, as she waited for Marco to come and join her, she *wanted* to be here. She wanted to go out with a smile and her head held high, not slink off into the darkness like a pet dog that had lost favour with its master.

Tomorrow she would leave, she determined, as the master arrived at her side. His hand came to rest against her back. His jacket sleeve brushed her bare arm. Her flesh began to tingle as she absorbed the impact of a pure male magnetism that never ceased to excite her, no matter what the mood between them was like.

Her chin was level with his shoulder, her eyes with his mouth. If she turned her head just a fraction she would be able to see the perfectly honed contours that made up his handsome face. But she didn't even need to move her head to pick up the tangy scent of him, because she was inhaling it with every breath that she took as they walked together towards the house.

Inside was awash with music and laughter. The moment they walked through the door it was like stepping into a different world. It came as a shock—the kind of shock that made Antonia pause and blink a couple of times in an effort to make the transition from hostility and darkness to merriment and light.

Then a cry of delight went up, and she saw their hostess separate herself from the group of people she had been with. In tow behind her was the man she had been married to for a year today.

Tall and dark, handsome and sleek, Franco de Maggio was very much of Marco's ilk. It should have made the two men natural rivals—but the truth was the opposite. They had known each other since kindergarten and been close friends ever since.

With her long black hair, stunningly beautiful dark brown eyes and dressed in slinky black crêpe that moulded her sensational figure, Nicola de Maggio was everything that Antonia was not. She was Italian, she had money in her own right, and her place beside Franco or another man like him had never been in any doubt from the day she had been born into her privileged life.

She belonged here. To Nicola, being a part of this society came as naturally to her as the inner warmth she exuded, which defied anyone not to instinctively like her simply for herself.

Antonia had liked her from the first moment they met, she as Marco's very new lover, Nicola as Franco's new bride. Liking had deepened into real affection since then. They were now good close friends—much like Marco and Franco. Yet Antonia had never ceased to be aware that she was the cuckoo in the nest.

Their smiles were genuine, their greetings were warm—and gave Antonia the excuse to move away from Marco's touch. On receiving their gift, their thanks were sincere. With a few teasing quizzes on what it might be, it was placed with all the other gifts waiting to be opened. 'It feels like our wedding day all over again,' Nicola sighed out happily. 'Wait until it's your turn, Antonia, and you will know just how blessed I feel.'

Marco stiffened, Antonia froze. Seeing their reaction, Nicola went quite pale. With a sharp glance at all three of them, Franco swiftly stepped into the breach. 'I think you should explain *how* blessed, *amore*,' he murmured softly, placing an arm around his wife's slender shoulders.

And it was a protective arm. An arm that said, It's okay. Not your fault. I'm here to smooth this out for you. Antonia wanted to run away, because it was as clear as day that Marco wasn't here to smooth anything out for her.

'We are going to have a baby!' Nicola suddenly announced in an anxiously rushed hush. 'Only we weren't going to say anything until later...'

She should be smiling, bubbling over with delight, but she couldn't because she was feeling so uncomfortable after what she'd said. So, pulling herself together, Antonia did it for her. 'Oh, that's wonderful news!' she exclaimed, and smiled—my God, how she smiled. She smiled as she hugged Nicola, and smiled as she kissed Franco's rather grim cheek. She even smiled up at Marco, though she wanted to hit him rather than smile at him.

His arm found her waist and he drew her close again. It was such a brave gesture, considering Nicola had just turned him to stone in horror. He even found a light rejoinder. 'Dinner next week,' he insisted. 'Just the four of us to wet the baby's head.'

I won't be here next week, Antonia thought, and smiled through that little knowledge also.

'You do that *after* the baby is born!' Nicola protested.

'Then we will wet the waiting *mamma's* head,' Marco compromised, and kissed the waiting *mamma's* now smiling mouth.

Between them all a nasty moment had been neatly smoothed over. Nicola was happy again, as she should be. Franco on the other hand looked curious as to what was going on between Marco and Antonia but was willing to hold his tongue.

Thankfully, a new bunch of latecomers arrived, giving the happy couple an excuse to escape. Once again, Antonia moved away from Marco's touch.

The worst of it was, he let her go.

So she threw herself headlong into the party to end all parties, as far she was concerned. For tomorrow I leave, was the chant playing over and over inside her head as she laughed and chatted happily away in Italian, the language being second nature to her, having spent the first five years of her life living here. And she danced, and ate very sparingly, and drank champagne by the glassful without knowing she was doing it.

Managing to corner her an hour later, Nicola demanded to know what was going on. 'If you two are avoiding each other like this because of what I said, then I am so sorry!' she cried. 'I can't tell you how awful I felt, setting you up in that dreadful way!'

'Don't be silly.' Antonia tried to smile it off—again. 'It really didn't matter.'

'If course it mattered,' Nicola insisted. 'I hurt you and infuriated Marco! He's barely speaking to anyone while you are partying as if this is your last night on this earth!'

Many a true word, Antonia thought bleakly. 'If Marco is still angry over an innocent remark, then shame on him and his overgrown ego,' she said. 'What did he think I was going to do? Jump in and ask him when I get to feel blessed?'

'You've lasted longer than any of his other lovers.' Nicola gently offered a phrase Antonia had grown very weary of hearing recently. Especially when it helped to mark that the end was most definitely nigh. 'That has to mean something, doesn't it?' Nicola pleaded.

Did it? 'It means I must be good at my job,' she provided, eyes hardening into cynicism. 'Do you think I'll be head-hunted when word gets around that I'm back on the market?'

Nicola's beautiful mouth dropped open. Across the room, standing by the drinks bar, Marco saw it happen and wondered what the hell Antonia had said to make Nicola gape like that.

Nothing nice, he concluded as he watched Nicola search the room until her eyes made contact with his. In a definite flurry, she looked quickly away again. And his senses were suddenly on full alert.

He didn't like this. He didn't like any of it. The whole damn day had gone from bad to worse, seemingly without him having any control whatsoever over it. Now something else was happening here that he didn't understand. Okay, Antonia was angry with him, he allowed. So he was a moody devil and probably deserved the way she was avoiding him like the plague. But whatever she'd just said to Nicola had been more than a complaint about his bad temper. His friend's wife had actually looked shocked and horrified.

Nicola was talking to her urgently—telling her that he was watching them, he realised, when Antonia turned so he could see the cold cast of defiance in her beautiful face. Their eyes made contact. If looks could kill, he'd be dead now, Marco acknowledged, and raised his glass to her in a silent toast meant to convey that he really didn't give a damn if she was hating him.

But it wasn't true. And that was his biggest problem where Antonia was concerned. Even now, while exchanging metaphorical knives across a crowded room, she lit him up so fiercely inside that if there was a polite way of doing it he would be getting her out of here and alone so he could demonstrate just how she affected him.

And that just about said it all as to why he was having these damned hard constant battles with himself. He wanted her. He *always* wanted her! Angry or not. Crowded room or not.

Why the hell should he give up something he still desired as much as this?

Almost as if on cue, the moment he planted that important point in his head, fate dealt him a lousy hand just to show to him that he wasn't the only person with a choice in this relationship.

A slight disturbance by the door caught Antonia's attention. She looked that way, Marco followed her gaze—then felt everything inside him close down completely when he found himself looking at none other than Stefan Kranst himself.

The moment Antonia saw him her beautiful face lit up, her gorgeous mouth broke into a sensational smile. And she struck out towards Kranst like a pigeon recognising home.

CHAPTER THREE

STANDING on the sidelines, Marco watched them meet, watched them smile, watched them murmur to each other. He watched Antonia lift her hand to his shoulders and Stefan Kranst slide his hands around her waist— then their mouths came together in a tender soft kiss.

He tried telling himself that it was just a greeting— that it was as natural as any other kiss exchanged tonight. But it wasn't true, and everyone knew it. Which was why conversations stopped, heads turned, and the whole room watched Marco Bellini's mistress embrace her ex-lover with brazen ease.

Strikingly tall and fair, Stefan Kranst might be ten years older than Marco, but he had as little trouble as Marco securing any woman of his choice. And *Dio*, he had secured a few during the year since Antonia had left him, Marco recalled deridingly.

But this woman was now *his* woman. She lived in his home, she slept in his bed, and she clothed herself with his money. Which made that lush red-painted mouth Kranst was kissing *his* exclusive property.

The primitive heat of an age-old burn of possessiveness began to form blisters inside the wall of his chest, the urge to go over there and drag them apart holding him absolutely still while he fought to contain such an utterly crass act. Everyone was watching, waiting— hoping, in their cruel little way, that he was going to do exactly that and cause the kind of nice juicy scene they could dine out on for the next month.

And her dress was too short, her legs too long, and her slender ankles too sexily elevated by the heels of her shiny-red backless shoes, Marco observed—refusing to remember that he had thought the exact opposite before he had witnessed her wrapped in that particular man's arms.

Had she done it for effect? Had she worn the dress because she'd known all along that Kranst would be here tonight and had wanted to please him? No bra, he remembered, dropping his eyes to the twin points of her breasts hovering a half centimetre away from Kranst's chest. He knew what that felt like. He knew what was happening to Kranst right now, because the bastard also knew what it felt like to hold Antonia that close.

No proper panties, either, knowing her. His eyes moved lower, checking for a tell-tale panty-line and finding none, which meant she was wearing one of those sexy little g-strings she liked to favour now and then.

Usually for his exclusive pleasure. So, when he saw Kranst's long artistic fingers splay over the slender curve of her hips, Marco took it as a personal insult to see her accept the intimacy as if the man still had every right to place his hands on her like that!

The sudden burst of soft laughter brought his hard gaze flicking upwards in time to catch that laughter animating just about every exquisite feature on her face. Then one of her hands curled around Kranst's nape, and they began talking to each other as if it was perfectly acceptable for them to behave like this in public.

But it was not acceptable, and she should know it. She should know that such behaviour with a man everyone here knew had been her lover before Marco only made her look cheap and made him look a fool!

Was she doing it deliberately? Was this her way of letting him know that he wasn't the only fish in her sea?

Sometimes he hated her. Sometimes he hated her so much he was bewildered as to how he could want her so badly, feeling the way he did. She wasn't his type. She had *never* been his type. She was too young, too uncultured and just too damn flighty! Or why else would she choose to stand out like an exotic flower in flimsy red silk while the rest of the room wore classy black chic?

Someone slid up beside him. 'Well, *caro*, she certainly knows how to make a man welcome,' a very mocking female voice drawled.

Gritting his teeth together behind the determinedly relaxed line of his mouth, Marco ignored Louisa Florenza's silken barb, and maintained his silence as the two of them stood watching Stefan Kranst begin edging Antonia backwards a few steps until he had put them both on the tiny dance floor.

Her hand remained curled around his nape. Both of his rested on her slender waist as he set them swaying to the music while they continued to talk. And their concentration on each other was so absolute that it was clear Antonia had completely forgotten all about the man she had actually come here with!

'You know, you cannot fail to be impressed by her complete lack of guile.' Louisa smoothly injected her next poisoned barb. 'Most women would be dying of embarrassment if they were confronted by their ex-lover in a room packed full of the friends of her present lover. But she doesn't seem to care at all!'

'You are standing next to me, *cara*,' Marco pointed out. 'Do you see me dying of embarrassment?'

As a reply, Louisa linked her arm through the crook

of his arm. 'We had some good times, Marco, hmm?' she murmured wistfully.

Good times? Watching Antonia swaying sensually to the music, he promised himself that if the gap between their bodies grew any smaller he would go over there and... 'You were a cat with claws, Louisa,' he drily reminded her. 'Which made the good times very few and far between.'

'I purred like a kitten in your bed, though,' she came back, with an example of that sensual purr.

It did nothing for him, which further annoyed him because it had used to do many things for him. But now all he could hear was another woman's soft sighs breathing tremulous pleas that could drive him out of his mind.

'And you liked to feel my claws now and again...'

'I still bear the scars,' he clipped.

'Good,' she said, but he sensed the knowledge getting through to her that his mind—and his body—was very much elsewhere right now. 'I hope you will always bear them. For what you are feeling now, as you watch her make love to him on the dance floor, is what I feel every time I see you with her. And those scars will last for ever, Marco, I can assure you.'

The bitterness in her tone finally caught his attention. Turning his head, he looked down into the face of one of Italy's most beautiful women—and smiled a very sardonic smile. 'Any scars you retain from me, *bella mia*,' he drawled, 'belong exclusively to the loss of that intravenous drip you had attached to my money.'

Unfazed by the accusation, Louisa held his very mocking gaze. 'Are you implying that *she* does not enjoy the same privilege?'

'No,' he conceded, and his smile began to tighten as

he returned his attention to the two closely linked bodies on the dance floor. 'But she has yet to abuse that particular privilege.'

'Clever girl,' Louisa commended.

Not so clever, Marco countered silently as he watched her soft-blonde head give a small shake that set the paste diamonds decorating the clasp holding up her lovely hair shimmering in the lights. Then she put her hand across Kranst's mouth to stop whatever it was he was saying to her.

Was he asking her to go back to him? Was he asking to paint her again? Was he talking sex to her just as Louisa was talking sex to him?

Intimacy was the absolute devil, he decided. A forsaken intimacy was even worse. It gave people you no longer felt a thing for a power over you you could never take back.

'He still wants her.' Louisa's remark hit him dead centre, as if she could tap into his thoughts.

'His desires don't interest me,' he answered dismissively. The real point was—did Antonia still want Kranst?

Then another thought slid silk-like into his head, filling him with something disturbingly like dismay. Could it be that Antonia was becoming tired of *him*?

The very suggestion was so alien to him that he couldn't quite work out how to handle it. No woman in his memory had even considered walking away from him until he was ready to let them go!

Then—no. Marco dismissed that idea with a contempt even he recognised as arrogance. She adored him. She always had done. If he walked over there right now and took her in his arms she would become his loving siren again within seconds, and Kranst would be the one left forgotten on the sidelines.

'He has the looks, *caro*.' Once again Louisa tapped into his thinking. 'He has the body and the reputation of a great lover. And although he may not have the social standing you possess, he can claim star quality, which cancels out the proud Bellini name. In fact,' she concluded tauntingly 'the only thing you seem to have that he doesn't are the financial resources you claim she doesn't abuse. But it is interesting how it always comes back to the money, hmm?'

Even to his own surprise, Marco released a burst of laughter. Because he was seeing the new red Lotus Antonia had walked past tonight as if it wasn't there. He was seeing a safe full of jewels she hardly ever asked to wear because she preferred to wear paste, like the clasp dressing her hair. And he was seeing an account in his own bank into which he paid a regular amount of money that she rarely spent.

So, no, avarice was not Antonia's besetting sin. But at least Louisa's peevish barb had put the humour back into his mood, so he repaid her by bending down to kiss her pouting mouth. She clung to him. He wasn't surprised—only indifferent—which was a shame, really, because Louisa would be his mother's idea of the perfect Bellini bride.

Shame—big shame—she wasn't his own.

'There,' Antonia declared. 'Didn't I tell you?'

Antonia was seeing that kiss Marco had just bestowed on Louisa Florenza as the final proof she needed to confirm that he was tiring of her.

'Men like Bellini do not replace old with older,' Stefan drawled sardonically. 'And you've just been kissing me,' he further pointed out. 'I would be flattered to think it was because you wanted me as your replacement lover, but we both know it wouldn't be true.'

'I love you more than anyone else on this earth, and I wish I'd never met him,' Antonia told him so tragically that Stefan had to sigh.

'My darling, the man is besotted with you. One only has to look at the too-cool way he is handling this little scene you're so carefully laying on for his benefit to know he's paying you back by doing the same to you.'

'If he loved me, he would be over here punching your lights out instead of laughing with her.'

'Well, thanks a lot,' Stefan drawled.

'It's all your fault, anyway,' she informed him churlishly. 'If you hadn't put my likeness into your stupid paintings, *he* wouldn't have bothered coming looking for me in the first place!'

'I didn't encourage you to fall for the rake.' It was Stefan's turn to laugh, and Marco's turn to listen to him doing it. 'You did that all on your own, Antonia. And I distinctly remember warning you off.'

It was such a painful little truth that she felt the tears suddenly flood into her eyes. Seeing them, Stefan released another sigh and pulled her just that little bit closer.

'You've been with him for over a year,' he gently reminded her. 'That's a whole lot longer than any other woman in his harem.'

'And the next person to tell me that will probably receive a slap,' she responded bitterly.

'But it still has to count for something, my darling,' he persisted. 'Can you honestly swear that he's actually said he no longer wants you?'

All Antonia did was smile cynically. For how many

hints did she need tossed at her to know what was going on inside Marco's head? Even the week in Portofino was beginning to look like their swan-song to her. They'd had a row a few days before, over his intention to spend several days with his parents on their Tuscany estate. And she'd taken offence that even after a year together he was still refusing to let her meet them. 'Anyone would think you were ashamed of me,' she'd said.

'My father is ill,' he'd replied. 'Show a little consideration for the plight of others.'

But he hadn't denied the accusation that he was ashamed. And his face had closed up, just as it always did when they touched on the subject of his exalted family. So he'd gone alone to Tuscany. She hadn't heard from him once in the three days he'd been there. And when he'd come back he'd been so moody and irritable that the sudden decision to spend a week together in Portofino had come as a complete surprise.

'That depends on your definition of *want*,' she said to Stefan with a bleak little smile. 'He still *wants* me in his bed, but out of it I just irritate the hell out of him.'

'Hence the hungry vamp act here with me, designed to *irritate* him even more so,' Stefan heavily concluded. 'Do you have a death wish or something, Antonia? Because, love you or hate you, Marco Bellini is not the kind of man you embarrass in front of his friends,' he warned very seriously. 'He'll strike back so hard you won't know what's hit you.'

From the corner of her vision she saw Marco join them on the dance floor with Louisa clasped in his arms. As Stefan swung her around she caught sight of Nicola standing watching them with anxious eyes while, beside her, Franco simply looked angry. And as it suddenly occurred to her that there was a lot of watchful tension eddying around in the atmosphere, she finally realised what had made Stefan issue the warning.

A calamity was brewing in Nicola's drawing room and, in her eagerness to score points off Marco's arrogant pride, she was unwittingly the cause of it.

'How did you manage to get an invite to this party?' she asked Stefan, suddenly realising that neither Franco or Nicola would be so insensitive as to invite him here, knowing his past relationship with their best friend's current mistress.

He smiled a brief smile. 'I came with Rosetta Romano,' he explained, naming the famous owner of the Romano Gallery in the Quadrilatero. 'I was good enough to step into the breach at short notice when her planned artist cancelled during a fit of temperament. So hawking me around Milan's most fashionable is her way of buying a bit of free advertising before the show opens.'

'Signora Romano obviously didn't know she would be causing one hell of a gaffe putting you, me and Marco in the same air-space,' Antonia said drily.

'Of course she knew.' Stefan grinned. 'How much free publicity do you estimate she'll get from setting up this potentially explosive scene?'

'And not just for the Romano Gallery,' she added, meaning that Stefan Kranst wasn't opposed to using notoriety to alert interest in his work.

His shrug was an arrogant acknowledgement of that. 'I'm a painter, not a diplomat. And anyway,' he added, looking into her eyes again, 'I wanted to see you, but trying to reach you through normal sources is virtually impossible. I've been leaving messages with your housekeeper all week, Antonia. Did you actually receive any of them?'

His meaning was clear. But Antonia shook her head at it. 'We've been away on a week's holiday,' she explained. 'And only arrived back late this afternoon. Today is the housekeeper's day off. I haven't seen Carlotta, had a chance to check messages or do anything other than get ready to come here.'

'So the guy hasn't resorted to censoring your messages yet?' He smiled a trifle cynically. 'I did begin to wonder when I couldn't get to speak to you personally,' he admitted. 'Because you can bet your sweet smile, my darling, that the moment I agreed to show in Milan, then Mr Patron of the Arts knew about it.'

He was implying that Marco had known about him being here in Milan and had deliberately kept the information from her! It seemed an appropriate moment for the music to stop. Stefan walked her to the edge of the floor and said nothing while she came to terms with the ugly possibility that he could well be right. For if anyone knew exactly what was happening on the art scene, here in Milan, then it was most definitely Marco!

The rat, she fumed. He might no longer want her for himself, but his inflated ego wouldn't sanction him having to witness her with a man who would *always* want her!

'Here.' Stefan offered her a glass of champagne. 'Drink this. You might feel better.'

Stubbornly dismissing the knowledge that she'd probably had more than enough champagne for one wretched night, she accepted the glass and drank the whole lot in a couple of determined gulps.

Champagne bubbles began to mix with anger in her blood. It was a dangerous combination. 'I think I hate him,' she announced with a deep sense of satisfaction for having said the words out loud.

'Well, in that case the next few minutes should be interesting,' Stefan murmured levelly. Dropping his eyes from a point somewhere over her left shoulder, he mocked her vehemence with a wry challenge. 'This may be a good moment for you to decide how much you hate him,' he suggested. 'Because war is about to be declared, my darling.'

He had to mean Marco, she realised, and felt the champagne bubbles start to pop. Her soft mouth parted, her eyes grew dark, and a helpless kind of indecision sent her hand out to swap her empty glass for his full one.

On a sigh, Stefan gave a shake of his head. 'You sweet idiot,' he murmured. 'Didn't it occur to you even once that *you* might not be ready for a showdown with him?'

An astute question, and a painful one, because she had considered and accepted only this morning that she wasn't ready for any kind of showdown with Marco. Now here she was, standing on the very threshold of one hell of a row—and in a room packed full of his loyal supporters.

Cuckoo in the nest didn't even cover what she suddenly began to feel like.

'Be brave, my friend,' Stefan softly encouraged. Then— 'Good evening, Marco.' He smiled. 'It's a pleasure to see you again...'

But it wasn't a pleasure for any of them. Standing close to Stefan still, Antonia was assailed by the familiar scent of Marco before she was assailed by the full impact of his physical presence. He arrived at her side, his shoulder level with her chin. As usual her skin began to shimmer at the near contact, her fingers curling tensely round the glass while she waited for him to say something totally unforgivable.

Yet all he did was offer Stefan his hand to shake and return the polite greeting without any obvious sign of animosity. 'You're showing at Romano's all next week, I believe.' As smoothly as that, Marco informed Antonia that he had known Stefan was here in Milan but had not bothered to tell her.

'The doors open on Saturday,' Stefan confirmed. 'I was just asking Antonia if you were both coming to my private viewing on Friday evening,' he added, with lying ease.

'And of course she assured you that we wouldn't miss it,' Marco returned in the same lying vein.

'Of course,' Stefan smoothly confirmed. 'Especially when I told her I have something for her to collect from me while she's there.' The smile at her puzzled frown and the teasing brush of a finger to her jutting chin were done, she was sure, simply to annoy Marco. 'Let's call it a belated birthday surprise,' he suggested. 'If you still have my *Mirror Woman*, Marco, then it may have some interest to you too,' he added lightly.

It was a baited hook.

'Sounds intriguing.' Marco smiled, but Antonia stiffened at the mention of the painting that had given Stefan his fame—and herself her notoriety.

She had only seen it once since the first evening she had arrived in Marco's apartment a year ago. The painting had been hanging in his study. When he'd shown it to her she hadn't been able to hide her dismay, because she hadn't realised that Marco actually *owned* the painting.

Marco had since moved it to a secure room connected to the study where he kept his more—personal investments.

Now Stefan was implying that he had another one just like it. And though she knew he was quite capable of producing a hundred paintings exactly the same, without needing the live model to do it, it disturbed her deeply to hear Stefan taunting Marco with the suggestion that he had returned to putting her in his paintings. Which led her straight to another question that set her trembling a little as she looked into his lean smooth indolently smiling face.

Had Stefan gone back on his promise to her?

Her eyes begged the question but Stefan refused to notice. Beside her Marco was playing it so casual she wondered if he even cared. But then, if she was on her way out, why should he care? she then asked herself. And, like this morning, she simply turned and walked away, with no stomach to play this game.

Only this time Marco didn't let her get far before his hand was capturing one of hers. She tried to tug free.

'Stop it,' he said, turning her round until he could see her face. Her eyes were too dark, her cheeks too pale, and her soft mouth was trembling. Marco knew the look, he knew she was hurting, but the knowledge that it wasn't him who had done the hurting this time didn't help to lighten his mood one little bit.

One part of him wanted to beat the hell out of Kranst for being so insensitive as to mention the *Mirror Woman*, when Marco was sure he must know the way it could upset her. While another part wanted to blast *her* to smithereens for still being so vulnerable to something she had, after all, posed for in all her naked glory!

'You reap what you sow, *cara*,' he told her grimly, took the glass from her fingers and put it aside, then pulled her the few steps needed to bring them onto the dance floor and folded her into his arms. 'Now dance,' he commanded, holding her close even while she tried to strain away from him. 'Remember where you are and who you will be hurting if you cause a scene here.'

As if on cue, Franco and Nicola danced in close to them. '*Ciao*,' Nicola greeted awkwardly. 'You two enjoying yourselves?'

She had to know that enjoyment was the last thing either he or Antonia were experiencing. 'We're having a wonderful time,' Antonia answered smilingly, coiling an intimate hand around Marco's neck—and dug her nails in. 'I love it when Marco comes over all macho.'

Franco flashed him a sardonic look, Nicola avoided eye contact completely. 'So long as you're happy,' their poor hostess mumbled, and looked relieved when her husband manoeuvred them away again.

'She hates scenes,' Marco sighed. 'She always has done.'

'I hate you,' Antonia responded. 'Does that mean I get a sympathetic sigh too?'

One part of him wanted to grin, the other part was furious. 'No,' he retaliated. 'You get to go home with the guy you hate and receive your just reward in private.'

With that he reached up and unclipped her nails, held onto the hand and trapped it between their bodies. 'Now look at me and smile,' he gritted. 'Or I think I might just kiss you senseless.'

If he expected the threat to subdue her, he soon learned otherwise when she had the absolute audacity to pull out one of her secret weapons that she kept under wraps for most of the time. Her head tipped backwards, her eyes grew sultry, and, setting the pink tip of her tongue between her even white teeth, she snaked up on her toe-tips and licked the thin line of his angry mouth.

Fire engulfed his body at the speed of lightning. Erogenous zones came alive with an urgency that stung.

Had she kissed Kranst like this? Made *him* feel like this?

Madre di Dio, he couldn't deal with the green streak of furious jealousy that went rampaging through him. 'We're leaving,' he announced.

'I want to stay,' she pouted, playing the seductress for all she was worth now, with sensual eyes and promising mouth and the inviting sway of her beautiful body.

In one corner of his consciousness he was totally engrossed in her, loving it—loving her defiance, her willingness to take him on, her deliberate public seduction. But another part was wondering if Kranst had incited this. With the flat of an angry palm pressed to her lower body he felt the smoothness of naked flesh beneath the clinging red fabric, and remembered Kranst's hand grazing the same area.

She quivered for him. Had she quivered for Kranst? From the periphery of his vision he could see Kranst standing there watching them. He felt a bloody black fury begin to throb with his heartbeat, and he bit out silkily, 'I'm game if you are.'

Lips gone so dry they were fused together, Antonia

felt the sheer heat of that challenge burn right down to her tingling toes. In any mood Marco was a breathtaking study of male beauty, but bad tempered and aroused he was awakening senses she hadn't known existed before she met him. Weak, sensual, female senses. The one which made man the aggressor and woman his more than willing slave.

She hated it—hated all of it.

'Okay,' she whispered unsteadily. 'We can leave...'

CHAPTER FOUR

THE drive back to the apartment was achieved in silence. Both tense, both angry for their own reasons. Both so sexually on edge that the atmosphere almost sizzled.

Antonia was out of the car even as Marco was still parking it. Making straight for the lift, she then committed the ultimate sin of not waiting for him before sending it up to the top floor. Having to kick his heels in the basement waiting for the lift to come back for him did nothing to improve his temper.

He arrived in the bedroom to discover that she had already locked herself into the bathroom. He could hear the shower running, and her red dress lay like a stain on the bright white tiling, the scrappy red shoes lying discarded beside it.

With frustration attacking him from all angles, he dragged off his jacket and had to really fight the temptation to slam it down beside the red dress and shoes in a counter-declaration.

It was realising the childishness in the act that made him stop to wonder bleakly what was happening to him. Anger, frustration, childish acts of temper? These were not the scenes he expected to fill his home with! They lacked the sophistication with which he liked to run his private life.

And, on top of that, he was beginning to feel like a jealous husband without the official bit of paper that said he had to put up with this. Hot anger suddenly turned to ice, the mere suspicion that Antonia was digging her claws into him deeply enough to make him feel that way, literally horrifying the heat out of him.

Marco was draping his suit jacket on a hanger when Antonia came out of the bathroom. Wide shoulders, long body, tight behind, powerful legs and a sleek olive hue to his skin that made her fingers itch to stroke it. She wished so much he had the face of a Gorgon to offset the perfect rest of him.

But he didn't. So when he turned to face her, even looking as coldly remote as he did, her body stirred beneath the silk robe she was wearing.

She wanted to hate him for being able to do that to her. Especially when all he did was freeze her with a look of contempt before turning away again.

'You've been working with Kranst again,' he declared flatly.

Without bothering to answer, she walked over to pick up the red dress and shoes from where she'd stepped out of them, and carried them over to the wardrobe next to the one he was standing by.

She opened one of the doors as he flicked one shut. 'Answer me,' he commanded coldly.

'I wasn't aware you'd asked a question,' she tossed back with equal cold. 'It sounded more like a statement of fact to me.'

From the corner of her eye she saw his mouth tighten, ignored the stinging warning in his eyes, and placed the shoes on the shoesrack before reaching up to pluck a hanger from the rail and begin hooking the thin shoulder straps of the dress onto it.

'Explain to me, then, what he was implying tonight, when he talked about something *interesting*.'

She shrugged as she re-hung the hanger on the rail.

'I have absolutely no idea.' Though she certainly had a few worrying suspicions.

'You must do,' Marco insisted. 'You know the man. You lived with him for over five years.'

Ten, she wanted to correct, but held back the information. 'And I've lived with you for all of one,' she pointed out as she closed the wardrobe door. 'But knowing what makes you tick is beyond me.'

'Oh, very trite,' he mocked. 'Now, answer my first question and tell me if you've been secretly working with him again.'

'For a man famed for the sharpness of his intelligence, you can be really dense sometimes,' she derided. 'Ask yourself—when?' she suggested. 'Have I had the opportunity to *work* or do anything else with Stefan?'

He didn't like the derision, his eyes darkened. 'For all I know the man might have a secret studio set up right here in Milan where the two of you meet on a regular basis.'

'So, I'm keeping the two of you happy?' Her laugh was scornful. But even Antonia was aware that her expression was suddenly guarded, because Marco had unwittingly drifted too close to a carefully kept secret of her own.

He saw the change. Of course he did. Reaching out with a hand, he drew her across the few feet separating them. His eyes were hard, his features grim and his grip on her wrist was firm. 'You're hiding something,' he gritted.

She refused to answer, her mouth set in a defiant pout. Marco formed his own conclusions, his expression darkening some more. 'If the two of you are plotting my embarrassment on Friday, then I'm warning you, you will regret ever knowing me!'

'Why won't you listen?' she snapped. 'I don't *know* what Stefan is planning for Friday!'

'Then why the shifty look?'

'You don't own the right to know my every secret!' she hit back bitterly. 'I'm your mistress, not your wife!'

This came hard on the fact that he had just reminded himself of the same thing, and his expression hardened into steel. 'The way the two of you were lost in deep conversation while you clung to him like a vine says to me that you were discussing something important while you made love to each other in front of everyone. And I want to know what that something is!'

'We were discussing you!' she flashed. 'And whether it was time for me to leave you or not!'

The claim had hit a nerve. Antonia actually saw it flick like the tip of a whip across his taut cheekbones. 'Are you saying he wants you back?' he demanded thinly.

'He will *always* have me back!' she flung at him recklessly. 'And when I'm ready to leave you, then I probably will go back to him!'

With that, she gave a tug at her wrist to free herself and walked proudly away, trying not to show how badly shaken she was feeling at this, the worst row they'd had to date.

Needing something to do in the drumming silence that followed her, she sat down on the stool in front of the dressing table and began to let down her hair.

'If there was the remotest possibility of you actually walking out on me, you would have done so without the warning,' Marco drawled in a voice loaded with derision.

'You think I'm a real push-over, don't you?' she muttered, tossing hairpins in an angry scatter across the dressing table top. 'You think that because you're as sexy as hell and so darn wealthy you can afford to buy anything, that I should be grateful that you decided to buy me!'

'I did not *buy* you,' he denied. 'I *chose* you. There is a definite difference between the two.' His arrogance, she noted, really showed no bounds. 'Whether or not you sold yourself to me, though, is a question I have no wish to hear the answer to.'

'Why not?' she challenged, via his reflection in the mirror. 'Are you afraid to discover that maybe your wealth is more appealing to me than your body?'

About to undo his bow-tie, she watched him stop and stiffen as if something really nasty had just stepped into the room. Antonia was very pleased to watch him do it. The man could be so insufferably conceited sometimes that it made her want to hit him where it would hurt the most!

'I sit here swathed in the finest silk,' she continued, to compound his momentary disconcertion, 'with my flesh pampered by the finest beauty products money can buy. I live in the kind of luxury most people only see between the pages of glossy magazines, and downstairs in the basement sits the kind of car most women only dream about owning—'

'The car belongs to me,' he inserted. 'You are merely permitted the use of it.'

'Permitted—!' A choked gasp brought her twisting round on the stool to stare at him. Then, 'Ah...' she said. 'So now we get down to the nitty-gritty. The car is yours. The luxury accommodation is yours. The expensive clothes I wear belong to you, as does the wonderful array of priceless jewels you keep carefully locked away in your safe until I require the use of them.

So—yes,' she acknowledged, 'I suppose it is natural for you to believe that I sold myself to you.'

'I never said that,' he snapped, a deep frown suddenly darkening his features as fresh irritation flicked into life.

'Then let's just clarify the point, shall we, so that it can be done with once and for all?' Getting up, she went to stand right in front of him. Confrontation wasn't in it. 'If, let's say, I decided to walk out on you right here and now, what would I be allowed to take with me?'

'This is stupid,' he sighed, sliding the strip of black silk out from under his shirt collar. 'When we both know you have no intention of walking anywhere.'

'The car? No,' she continued, regardless. 'The jewels? Definitely no. What about all the designer clothes, then? Have I performed well enough to earn the right to take those, Marco?' she questioned provokingly. 'Or do you intend to let me walk out on you naked? If so,' she added, without giving him a chance to answer, 'then you surely can't say that I sold myself to you. For what exactly is it I am supposed to have gained from doing so?'

'A year of great sex?' he suggested nastily.

'Oh,' she pouted. 'I was hoping you would have the good taste to leave the sex thing out of this.'

'Why?' he asked tauntingly. 'When it is all I—'

Marco stopped himself—but not soon enough. And the black anger went flooding through him again as he watched her annoyingly provocative face blanch.

'You asked for that,' he insisted, wishing to hell he had never started this.

'Yes,' she agreed, 'I surely did.' But the fight had disappeared from her tone, and his jaw felt so tight it was in danger of snapping.

She went to turn away from him. It was sheer frustration with the whole sordid scene that made him stop her, he told himself. It had nothing to do with the sudden suspicion that if he let her turn away she would never turn back to him again.

So his hands found her shoulders and drew her against him, then, simply because he needed to do it, he lowered his head and his mouth took her mouth by storm.

At least she didn't fight him, but neither did she respond. She just stood limp and lifeless against his body while his mouth ravaged hers without receiving any feedback at all.

Not liking what was happening here, and liking even less the knowledge that she could stand there lifeless while his own body was reacting as fiercely as it always did to her, he went for the kill with a pride-staking vengeance aimed at demolishing her resistance.

For he knew this woman, he consoled himself grimly as he began covering her face with the kind of small light teasing kisses guaranteed to drive her wild. Her cheeks, her jaw-line, her firmly closed eyes, the length of her small straight nose. His kisses found all the right pleasure points while carefully avoiding her mouth even when, with a helpless whimper, she slackened its tense little line in sensual expectation.

Yes, he confirmed triumphantly. He knew her so well. The way her breathing quickened, and she began to vibrate to the feather-light stroke of his fingers. It was easy to urge the silk from her shoulders and leave it to slither down her body until the only thing holding it up was the belt knotted around her waist.

As she released a gasp in startled surprise he at last captured her mouth again. She fell into his kiss like a woman with a fever. When her fingers came up to clutch at his rock-solid biceps, he stroked her hair, stroked her body, and stroked her beautiful breasts with their sensitive points that simply begged for his further attention.

He gave it willingly, knowingly—ruthlessly, arching her over his arm so far that she had no choice but to reach up and hook her hands around his neck to maintain some control over her own balance.

Within seconds she was groaning. Eyes closed, head tilted right back so her long silken hair swung in a rippling swathe over his arm as he grimly tore through every veil of rejection she had dared to pull on against him. When the groans became hot little gasps of pleasure, he consolidated his success by gliding a hand along a silken thigh until it found the cluster of golden curls that shrouded her sexuality. The robe was no barrier; it had already slid apart to give him easy access. But the real triumph came when her thighs parted for him in all-out invitation.

The battle, in his mind, was surely over. Having won it, as abruptly as he had started it, he brought it to an end and watched with a grim detachment as she leaned weakly against him, dizzy and disorientated enough to find it impossible to support herself.

'You want *me*, Antonia,' he declared in a tough cold voice that made her shiver. 'Try dangling another man in front of me in an effort to improve on what we have, and you will find yourself having to learn not to want.'

It was an outright warning.

Standing there in his arms, Antonia said absolutely nothing. He'd done this to her merely to make a point. It was humiliating.

After a moment, he sighed and let go of her. She swayed a little, but found her balance, and remained exactly as she was while he strode for the door. And what was the picture he took with him? Antonia asked herself as she watched him go.

His suitably chastened mistress standing there with her seduction-red silk robe still hanging from her waist by the belt, and her breasts still taut and alive and throbbing. Like her mouth—like her sex.

She had never felt so sickened in all her life.

Sickened by herself—sickened by him. Sickened by the knowledge that really they were both as bad as each other. For Marco might take and take and take, but she had let him do it.

'I hate you,' she whispered, not sure if she was telling herself that or the wretched man striding out of the door.

Whichever, he heard it, paused and turned. There was contempt in that lean hard handsome face of his. Enough contempt to make her skin crawl.

'Take my advice, *cara*, and think carefully about on which side your bread is buttered. Beautiful women come in disposable packs of ten these days.' The cut of his cynicism was deep enough to draw blood. 'A poor performer can therefore be tossed onto the scrap heap and replaced as easily as—that.'

The snap of his long brown fingers made her flinch. Marco gave a curt nod of his dark head to acknowledge it, then left the room.

But he took with him the sight of her standing there still half stripped of her robe. It made him sigh again as he slammed into his study. For, no matter how ruthlessly he had just set out to demolish her, the way she had refused to cover herself seemed to give her the last word that was strangely demolishing *him*.

What was it exactly he had been trying to prove? he

asked himself as he made directly for the whisky bottle. That she *had* to love him more than she loved Kranst?

She'd left the handsome bastard for him, hadn't she? Marco argued with his own angry head. And why bring the love thing into it when he had never asked or wanted love from any woman?

But neither do you want to believe she could have the capacity to love another man, his conceited side answered the question. You're an arrogant swine, Bellini, he told himself. You want it all. You always have done. But you're never going to give that much back in return.

Snatching up the bottle and a glass, he took them over to his desk then threw himself down into the chair. Whisky splashed into the glass. He tipped it down his throat, swallowed, then sat back to glower darkly at nothing.

He'd never felt like this before, and he didn't want to feel like this now! Angry and guilty and—yes, he admitted it—riddled with confusion and jealousy. It creased his insides every time he heard Kranst's name leave her lips in that oh, so tender way she always said it. And seeing her clinging to the man tonight had forced him to trawl whole new depths of jealous resentment.

'He still wants her,' Louisa had said.

Well, so do I!

Another splash of whisky burned its way down to his stomach.

And he wasn't giving her up just to watch her walk straight into the arms of her ex-lover as if Marco Bellini had never even been there!

Was that it? he thought suddenly. Was that what was really bugging him? The idea that if he did send her packing she would simply go back to where she had been before she met him and pick up where she'd left off, with hardly a tear to say she was sorry to do it?

To hell with Kranst. Antonia was *his* woman! And Kranst could go and look elsewhere for his inspiration.

Which reminded him about the painting the guy had been taunting him with tonight. Getting up, he staggered, frowned down at the whisky bottle, and was amazed to discover how much of it had gone.

Drunk. He was drunk. Well, that was a first since his reckless youth, he thought with a grimace. Would Antonia be pleased to know what she had driven him to?

Concentrating on walking in a straight line, he went over to a door and punched a set of numbers into the security console, heard the lock shoot back and pushed the door open on the investment side of his art collection—the Rembrandt, the Titian, the Severini and the Boccioni, which his insurers insisted he kept housed in a secure room.

Would Antonia be pleased to know what else he had in here? he mused as, with glass in hand, he walked right past the masters, his attention fixed only on Stefan Kranst's *Mirror Woman*.

It was only one of a series the artist had produced over several years. Each painting was different, but the theme was always the same—perfection seen through the eyes of the artist via a mirror reflection.

What had Kranst really been trying to say when he'd painted Antonia like this? Marco pondered thoughtfully. That the mirror reflected her perfection where reality did not? Or had Kranst merely been the voyeur, capturing on canvas something he knew he could never have any other way?

Marco frowned as he always did when he tried to understand what Kranst had been trying to relay here. No suggestion he could come up with ever truly fitted. The idea of Kranst as the mere voyeur, for instance, was shot to pieces the moment you saw the two of them together. They *knew* each other *intimately*. Touch, taste, sight, sound. In fact he had never experienced intimacy like it between two people, unless he included himself with her.

As for the mirror-perfection versus reality: the painting didn't lie. Antonia was as perfect in real life as Kranst had portrayed her here.

The *Mirror Woman* was easily the best of the series—which was why Marco had bought it. It was also the most disturbing, because this was the only painting where Antonia stood in full focus. She was standing on a balcony—an *English* balcony, he mused with a grimace. Long and slender, naked and sleek, with an early-morning sunrise caressing her skin with pale gold silk. She was looking back over her shoulder towards the mirror with a terrible—terrible sadness in her beautiful eyes.

Frowning, he reached out to absently graze a fingertip over an unusually careless brush-mark blemish that shouldn't be there on her left shoulder. Then her eyes were drawing his attention again. Those dreadful, empty, haunted eyes. What was she supposed to be seeing when she looked into the mirror like that? Herself? The artist? Something else unseen by anyone else from this angle?

He'd once asked Antonia why the look. 'Life,' she'd answered flatly. 'She's seeing life.' Then she'd shuddered and walked away and never asked to see the painting again.

It had been an unexpected response from someone who refused to reveal any hint of embarrassment whenever she came up against her own nudity in one of the many other forms it had taken since Kranst had painted her. The signed prints, the calendars, greetings cards, etcetera, being the mediums by which the artist earned his real fame and fortune.

Only this painting upset her. Or was it the fact that *he* owned it that made her walk away? She refused to talk about it, and would be appalled to find out that to acquire it he'd had to convince his own mother to sell it to him.

The irony in that put a smile on his lips. 'Stefan Kranst is a worthy investment,' his mother had said. 'He has a gift for catching the inner soul of his subject. This poor creature, for instance, is dying inside that beautiful outer casing. I feel for her. I feel for the artist because he so clearly loves the inner woman.'

The word *dying* was a disturbing description. He preferred the word *empty*, because it soothed some part of him to know that Antonia had never looked empty while she had been with him.

But his mother had admired the woman in the painting *before* she had known Antonia had moved in with him. Now all she saw was a woman willing to expose herself for all to see and who possessed no conscience about doing it. She also despaired, because her son had not yet assuaged what she saw as his obsession with both the painting and the woman.

The smile turned itself into a sigh, because he was aware he hadn't assuaged anything where Antonia was concerned. Not his desire for the woman or his fascination with this painting.

Now Kranst was implying that there was another

painting, like this one. Which meant what, exactly? That Kranst hadn't painted out *his* obsession with Antonia? That this new painting was going to tell him things he didn't want to know?

If that was Kranst's motive, then Marco didn't want to find out, but he knew he needed to. He didn't want to go to Kranst's damned private viewing, but he would have to go.

And he didn't want to lose Antonia, but he had a horrible feeling he was going to lose her one way or another. By his own stupid actions or with the help of exterior forces like Kranst or his mother or the compelling pull of his sick father's need.

The whisky no longer had any flavour. The painting of Antonia suddenly did nothing for him. He wanted the real woman. The one he had just hurt for no other reason than a need to reassure his own ego.

But she was *still* the warm and pliant woman probably lying fast asleep in his bed now, he then added, with yet another kind of smile as he left the room and closed the door behind him. Then, with a walk that was almost unwavering, he rid himself of his glass and went to join her.

The bedroom was in darkness, the bed a mere shadow on the other side of the room. Making as little noise as possible, he stepped into the bathroom, silently closed the door to spend a few minutes trying to shower off the effects of the whisky, before going back into the bedroom and over to the bed.

He meant to surprise her awake with some serious kisses in some very serious places. She would be sulking, of course, but he could deal with that. She would fight him too, he would expect nothing less. And he would grovel a little because she deserved to have him grovel—before he drowned himself in the sweetest pleasure ever created for a man to share with a woman.

Then he stopped and frowned when he found himself staring down at the smooth neatness of an untouched bed.

CHAPTER FIVE

A SHAFT of alarm went streaking down his backbone and massed deep in his abdomen. He spun, sharp eyes piercing the darkness to scan the room for a sign of her shadowy figure—curled in a chair, maybe, or standing by the window.

She wasn't there. The alarm leapt up to attack his heartbeat. She wouldn't, he told himself. She couldn't have quietly dressed and left him while he'd been busy drowning his sorrows—could she?

No, he wouldn't have it. He might have behaved like a rotten bastard, but Antonia would never just walk out and leave!

But then there was Kranst waiting on the sidelines, he remembered, and started moving, unsure, so damned unsure of himself that the uncertainty was actually making his legs feel hollow with fright!

It was the whisky, Marco told himself. But he was still going to kill her when he found her for scaring him like this, he vowed, as he began striding round the apartment opening doors and closing them until he came to the locked door belonging to one of the spare bedrooms.

Relief shuddered through him, followed by a shaft of white-hot fury at her whole attitude. Stubbornly forgetting his own bad behaviour. he banged hard on the door. 'If you don't unlock this door I'll break it down!' he shouted threateningly.

And kept on banging until the door flew open.

Antonia was already walking away from it even as it swung back on itself. Her hair rippled about her naked shoulders and his body almost screamed as it responded to the carelessly sensual sway of hers. And it was the turn of the red silk wrap to lie in a discarded blot on the floor.

'Don't ever lock me out of a room in my own home again,' he ground out as he strode forward.

'I have nothing to say to you,' she replied in a voice meant to freeze a man's nether parts.

A willingness to grovel was forgotten—ousted by a much more satisfying desire to remind her just who called the tune around here.

Arriving at the bed, she prepared to climb back into it. In two long strides he stopped her, by the economical act of scooping her off her feet. Her protesting shriek was ignored, as were her wriggling attempts to get herself free. Without a single word from his tightly clamped lips, he turned and began carrying her out of this bedroom and down the hall to *his* bedroom.

'You are such a primitive underneath the layers of breeding,' she sliced at him disgustedly.

He stopped dead and kissed her—so hot and so hard she was gasping for breath by the time he lifted his head again.

'Is that primitive enough?' he asked, not in the least bit insulted she'd called him that. In fact he liked the whole scenario, since he was feeling very primitively aroused right now.

Marco shut the door behind them with a very satisfyingly primitive kick. The bed waited. He dumped her on its pale blue cover, then followed with the long hard length of his body in a very primitive man-on-top-of-woman pinning down.

Her angry eyes shot amber bright warnings at him. Her beautiful hair streamed out above her head, and her clenched fists made a puny but determined effort to do him some damage. 'Get off me,' she insisted. 'You're just a big brute—*and* you taste of whisky!'

'And you taste of champagne and woman—*my* woman,' Marco growled back, enjoying this new primitive role that allowed him the rare luxury to completely dominate.

Her breasts heaved against the solid wall of his chest and her slender hips writhed delightfully beneath the pressure of his. She felt the rise of his passion and spat her utter contempt at him, while the mocking arch of his eyebrows asked her who was to blame.

She hit back with more than her fists, 'Stefan was right about you,' she lashed. 'You are a—'

Ducking between the flailing fists, he stopped the words with his mouth. Discussing Kranst was *not* going to happen in *his* bed! he grimly determined, and kept on kissing her until her hands stopped punching and began to anxiously knead his shoulders instead.

Triumph sizzled through his system; the red-hot heat of desire spun through his blood. He made love to her as if there was no tomorrow and, because there was still the heat of an angry fear burning behind the passion, he drove her to the edge more than once before ruthlessly drawing back again.

'I hate it when you do this to me,' she sobbed in frustration.

'You would hate it more if I didn't do it at all,' he threw back.

Her breath broke on a whimper because she knew he was right. The helpless little sound did things to him no woman could ever begin to understand. He thrust into her with the force of absolute possession.

'You belong to *me*. Just remember that next time you feel like wrapping yourself around another man.'

If he'd expected her to respond at all, it was not the way she did. With the slick roll of her body he suddenly found he was the one pinned down and she the one most definitely on top. For the next few minutes he experienced what it was like to be utterly seduced by a woman hell-bent on making him embarrass himself.

It didn't happen. He was no one's easy victim. But Antonia in this mood was irresistible. She was the true sensualist born to pleasure man. She kissed him and stroked him and rode him towards heaven. And when his body began to tighten and his heart began to pound, she gave him back a taste of his own medicine by pulling away to rise up and stand over him.

Feet planted either side of his body, hands resting in the delicious groove of her slender waist, and her wonderful long golden hair spiralling around the face of an absolute wanton, she asked, 'And who do *you* belong to, Marco?'

The little minx. The beautiful, outrageous little minx! he thought, and, with a laugh of appreciation, he jack-knifed into a sitting position, clamped his hands to her hips—and gave his mouth the pleasure of bringing her to heel again.

The battle progressed to a different level. She gasped and protested and tugged at handfuls of his hair in an effort to dislodge him, and eventually lost the ability to stand. She was groaning and trembling but still in there fighting, matching him kiss for kiss, caress for caress, intimacy for exquisite tortuous intimacy, which had them crossing a few boundaries they'd never attempted to cross before in their quest to get the better of the other.

By the time he was back where he belonged—on top and deep inside her—he had lost the will to pull back again. Hot, bathed in sweat and no longer on this planet, they rode the fiery dragon with a focused compulsion that blocked out everything else.

He climaxed first—she was so damned determined to make him do that. But she followed a half-second later, urging him on with the convulsing tug of her muscles towards the kind of prolonged orgasm that laid them both to waste for long minutes afterwards.

Yes! he thought with a deep satisfaction as he lay heavy on her, fighting for breath. This was it, the elixir of life, and to hell with the covetous Kranst. To hell with his disapproving mother! he added fiercely to that—he couldn't bring himself to repeat the dismissive curse regarding his father, but inside he was aware that the need to hold on to what he had here was beginning to overshadow everything else.

Lying there beneath him, almost completely engulfed in his body and his scent and the glorious weight of his utter satiation, Antonia wondered ruefully if she would ever find the energy to move again. Her bones felt like liquid and certain muscles were trembling in the aftermath of something pretty spectacular, even for them.

What she couldn't understand was how it could be like that after what had gone before it. She should have been repulsed by his touch. She should have lain like a stone beneath him. But she hadn't—she hadn't....

Weak, you're weak, she derided herself miserably, and made a move to remind him that she was still here, just in case he'd forgotten while he basked in sexual bliss.

With a kiss to her brow, he acknowledged her presence, then relieved her of his weight by rolling them onto their sides so he could wrap her against him.

'You move me like no other woman,' he murmured huskily.

Did he think that was a compliment? she asked herself. Because it wasn't. She had no wish to be tagged and sorted according to performance. In fact, if she had the energy she would take serious offence and get up and leave!

But she didn't have the energy. And, in truth, lying here against him in the soft darkness of the summer night, with one of his hands gently stroked the curve of her hip while the other absently grazed over her left shoulder, she could think of no other place she would rather be.

Weak, she repeated. It was her biggest problem. She needed to be with him though she didn't *want* to need. He was arrogant, self-motivated, insensitive and...

Her sigh warmed his throat. Dipping his dark head, he caught the sigh with the kind of kiss that squeezed the heart dry. When it was over she reached up to touch his lips with her fingertips, unable to believe that a mouth could be so tender and not feel something deeper than desire for her.

'I wish I'd never met you sometimes,' she quietly confided.

'Only sometimes?' he threw back.

Tipping her head, she expected to find him smiling. But he looked quite sombre as he gazed down at her through swirling smoke-blue eyes set between kohl-black lashes in a polished bronze framework no gifted sculptor could improve upon.

'Do you want me to apologise for my earlier behaviour?' he asked her. Huskily spoken, sincerely meant. No, she thought sadly. I want you to love me. Then had to swallow the lump of tears in her throat as she gave a shake of her head. 'I just want you to promise never to do that to me again,' she replied.

Smoke-blue eyes darkened with repentance. 'On my life,' he vowed, and sealed it with a kiss, then repeated it again and again until both the vow and the kiss became yet another seduction.

It was his way, a willingly humble side to his proud character, which had the power to demolish her resistance far more easily than the ruthlessness he had meted out before.

Her fingers began trailing tender caresses across hair-peppered, muscle-hard, satin-tight flesh. He was built to worship, she thought mistily. Built to make any woman melt with desire. It was she who deepened those soft penitent kisses into one long sensual banquet. She who slid onto her back and drew him over her, then slowly relaxed her thighs so he would settle between. In a wonderful intimacy that had her long legs tangling with his and her body arching to a sensual rhythm, they indulged in a different kind of kiss.

His mouth left hers to taste other parts of her, and she sighed in pleasure as it closed on her breast. Fingers trailed into his hair, stretched out to glide down the satin smoothness of his back. He shuddered in response and drew on her nipple until she felt the needle-sharp pleasure reach deep down into her very core.

As quickly as that, it all began again. No tormenting this time, no battle of wills. In only seconds he was feeding his powerful arms beneath her so he could lift her into closer contact with the pulsing length of his sex.

Dragging his mouth from her breast, he requested, 'May I?'

'Oh, yes,' she invited, aware that they were both more than ready for this.

This time he came into her with the gentle force of a man who was very mindful of his own power. She willingly accepted him, and wasn't surprised to hear them both utter those exquisite sighs of pleasure because, quick though this was, they were perfectly in tune.

Can I walk away from him? Antonia found herself questioning as not just her senses but her whole world began to quicken. Can *he* really want this to end?

As if he could sense that her mind had strayed, Marco was suddenly rearing up and over her. His eyes were like two dark circles of passion, his mouth warm and moist and hungry for hers. 'This is special,' he said roughly. 'And it is ours.'

'Sometimes it feels as if you hate me,' she whispered.

'No, never,' he denied, and crushed her mouth beneath his and crushed all thoughts from her head by other means.

The next morning, the light brush of his lips on her cheek awoke her. Opening her eyes, she smiled sleepily at him.

Clean-shaven and smelling deliciously vital, he was already dressed for his busy day in a dark grey suit and pale blue shirt that did sensational things to his golden features.

'Get up, get dressed and come and join me for breakfast,' he invited. 'I have a surprise for you.'

'A surprise?' she repeated, yawning while stretching.

'Mmm,' he murmured, and it was the sexiest murmur Antonia had ever heard in her entire life.

It brought an invitation to her eyes and a hand reaching up for him. 'Show me now,' she commanded in a tone which was demanding something else entirely.

He caught the hand, kissed it, then firmly replaced it back on the bed. 'Not on your life.' He grinned. 'You have to come downstairs looking prim for this surprise.'

And with that thoroughly intriguing statement he turned and strode out of the room. Antonia watched him go with a smile in her eyes, quietly amazed at how a night of loving could turn their relationship around. The man was an enigma of complicated mood codes: one minute looking as if he wished to see the back of her, the next almost dying with pleasure in her arms. Now he wanted to please her with surprises—though how he'd found the time to come up with anything to surprise her with at—she checked the bedside clock—seven o'clock in the morning was completely beyond her.

Innovative, that was what Marco was, she thought indulgently as she climbed out of the bed and went off to shower and dress, as instructed, in something prim. Her choice was a white tailored linen suit teamed with amber accessories that almost matched the colour of her eyes.

On her way to the breakfast room, she popped her head into the kitchen and was surprised to find no housekeeper there to exchange the usual morning greetings. Still frowning slightly at Carlotta's absence, she entered the sunny breakfast room to find her favourite breakfast bowl of fresh fruit and a steaming pot of hot coffee waiting for her on the table—and her favourite man reclining in his chair reading his morning newspaper.

But he paused to watch her walk towards him with his eyes narrowed in male appreciation. '*Perfezione*,' he murmured, as she leant down to press a morning kiss to his ready lips.

'*Grazie*,' she returned in mocking relief. 'For this is about as prim as I get.'

The sun caught the strawberry highlights threading through her neatly pleated hair, and played sultry games with the amber colour of her conservatively styled silk blouse. On her feet she wore classically plain court shoes and a simple string of pearls she had owned for ever and didn't warrant locking away in Marco's safe circled her slender throat. Her make-up was so natural there was barely any sign of it and her smile said everything was right in her world.

'Where's Carlotta?' she asked as she sat down next to him.

'Called in sick,' Marco explained. 'I found her message waiting with our answering service, along with a hundred and one others…'

Antonia's hand froze momentarily on its way to pick up the coffee pot. Stefan, she remembered. Stefan had said he'd been leaving messages for her all last week. A small silence began to vibrate with the hum of expectancy while she waited for what Marco was going to say next.

But he said absolutely nothing, and when she dared a glance at him, he was behind his newspaper again. He wasn't going to mention Stefan's calls, she realised. And she was damned if she was going to mention them and put at risk all this wonderful harmony they had managed to recapture.

So, 'Did Carlotta say what was wrong?' she enquired instead.

The newspaper twitched, long brown fingers flexed slightly, as if he was aware that she was aware of Stefan's calls and those fingers were reacting to the fact that she too was going to pretend they had never happened.

'Summer flu,' he replied. 'She does not wish to pass it on, so she expects to be away for the rest of the week.'

'Poor Carlotta. I must send her a get-well card,' she murmured, and finished pouring her coffee before transferring her attention to her bowl of fruit. 'Did you prepare this?' she asked.

'Mmm.' It was not quite the sexy *Mmm* of before. Was he angry? Was he annoyed that she wasn't going to ask about Stefan's calls?

'Molti grazie, mi amante,' she returned, determinedly keeping her tone light. 'This unusual act of servility is most definitely your biggest surprise to date.'

The husky dark tones of a very male laughter flipped her heart over, then it flipped again with relief when he folded the paper away and she was able to see the humour also reflected on his beautiful face.

He wasn't brooding about Stefan. He wasn't going to let this newly attained harmony spoil because of a few silly messages. 'Eat your fruit. Drink your coffee,' he advised indulgently. 'We have approximately ten minutes before we have to leave.'

'Leave?' She frowned. 'Why? Where are we going?'

'I'm going to Venice,' he replied as he got to his feet. 'And you, *mi bellisima*, are coming with me.'

With that, he dropped a casual kiss onto the top of her head and began to stroll arrogantly for the doorway.

But this time no warm smile followed him. No feeling of delight that he was planning to take her along on one of his business trips for the first time since she'd entered his life.

So much for protecting harmony, she mused grimly as she felt it all wither away. 'When did you decide this?' she fed quietly after him. 'Before or after you played back the messages?'

He stopped walking and turned, an almost saturnine figure with his features suddenly cast in bronze. 'Before,' he replied, earning himself a flash of scepticism. 'It was learning that Carlotta would not be around to play chaperon that clinched your fate for you,' he answered that scepticism. 'For no woman plays Marco Bellini false while he is safely ensconced elsewhere, *capisce*?'

Oh, she understood all right. He didn't trust her to be alone in Milan with Stefan in the same city. 'So the surprise you promised was never intended as a pleasant surprise,' she concluded, and smiled cynically. 'How typical of you to give with one hand and take back with the other.'

'On the contrary,' he argued. 'The trip to Venice could be a pleasure for both of us. It really depends on whether you want to make it so.'

'Or not, if I decide to stay here instead,' Antonia pointed out.

The threat had him walking back to her. When he reached her side, he bent to place one hand on the back of her chair, the other flat on the table. The way he loomed over her hinted at menace. Placing her fork in the bowl of fruit, Antonia refused to let her fingers shake as she placed them down on her lap, then sat back in the chair to face his hard gaze squarely.

'You prefer to stay here?'

His eyes held hers, and were loaded with challenge. Answer *yes* and she would be lying, not to mention confirming his suspicions about her motives. Answer *no* and she would be feeding his ego with something she had no wish to feed him now.

She went for the compromise. 'Stefan is my *friend*. Why can't you accept that?'

His eyes didn't waver, not for a second. 'Do you prefer to stay?' he repeated.

Hers did, though; they flickered away on a frown of irritation. 'Of course I would rather be with you,' she sighed. 'But not under duress, and *not* because you feel it's your only option!'

'I could throw you out. That's another option.'

'I could walk!' she lashed back. 'That's an even better one!'

'Are you coming?' The wretched man wasn't fazed in the slightest.

'Yes!' she snapped, and dislodged his hand by pushing back her chair and shooting to her feet with a jolt of anger.

He just sent her a mocking look. 'Then eat your fruit and drink your coffee,' he suggested, and with a wave of a hand walked away again. 'Come and get me from my study when you're ready to leave.'

'I'll need longer than ten minutes to clear up here before we go,' she threw impatiently after him.

'For you, *mi amante*, I will delay our flight!'

Magnanimous in victory, he left her standing there not sure whether to smile or scowl. The smile won, twitching impulsively at the corners of her mouth as she sat down to finish her fruit. Twenty minutes later she was annoyed again because he hadn't told her until just before they were leaving that they were going to stay over in Venice, so she hadn't bothered to pack a bag.

'Shop for what you need when we get there,' said the man to whom money had a different meaning.

'For want of a further five minutes it seems terribly extravagant,' she complained.

'Time is money to me, *cara*,' he pointed out.

'Then I'm sorry for costing you money while you waited,' she said primly. 'What a problem I am to you.'

Sarcasm or not, he slashed a grin at her. 'My biggest problem is going to be keeping my mind on business when I know you're within easy reach of me,' he murmured lazily.

'Then I hope you spend your meetings in a state of permanent distraction.'

'While you do what?'

'Spend your money as fast as I can produce the credit cards,' she answered.

He laughed, and kissed her until the lift arrived. After that it didn't really matter any more that he was only doing this to keep her and Stefan apart. The harmony was back, and she was happy to bask in it. Happy to bask beneath the amount of care and attention he paid her throughout their short flight to Venice and the ensuing journey along the canals until they came to their hotel.

Heads turned, people stared. She basked in that also. For being with a man like Marco Bellini was a bit like walking alongside royalty: paths were smoothed, people deferred. He was rich, he was known, he was handsome and single. Women envied her place in his life. Men envied all his many advantages.

Having safely delivered her to their hotel, he left her to her own devices while he went off to keep his appointments. She shopped till she'd dropped, and spent the rest of her time trailing around some of the tourist sites amongst the thick summer crowds and the heat that melted.

By the time she arrived back in their suite she was so exhausted it was all she could do to run a bath and sink into it. On the bed lay the smart designer bags to go with her new smart designer purchases. On the floor lay the scatter of her discarded clothes.

Letting himself in a few minutes later, Marco smiled at the evidence of her occupation. Antonia was untidy by nature, though she would make the effort to try not to be because she thought it must irritate him. Being brought up to strict rules set by a succession of nannies meant that regimental neatness had become second nature to him.

But it didn't irritate him. In truth, he liked to walk into a room and see instant proof of her presence. The bathroom door stood ajar, and from behind it he could hear the lazy slap of water which told him what she was doing now.

It was the easiest thing in the world to strip off his clothes and go in there to join her. Up to her neck in bubbles, she smiled as he approached, lifted her knees to allow him room to sit down opposite her, then, on a contented sigh fed her feet up his chest as he stretched his long legs on either side of her.

'Long day?' he enquired.

'Spent your money. Played tourist. Got too hot. Killed my feet. Came back here to die peacefully. And you?' she returned the enquiry.

'Made a few lira, invested a few lira.' His accompanying shrug said it was par for the course. 'Threw my impressive weight around a bit. Came back here to make love to this woman I know.'

Her eyes began to gleam. 'Is she any good?'

So did his. '*Molti bellisima*,' he softly confided, and picked up one of her feet to begin an expert massage to its slender sole. She liked that. Closing her eyes, she simply lay back and let him indulge her.

In fact Marco indulged her in many ways during the next few days. They dined in quiet out-of-the-way places where the tourists didn't go, walked hand in hand through narrow streets like dark caverns, and made love for most of the night. When he had to leave her to attend his meetings he made it brief, and secondary to what was really going on here in Venice.

Which was the steadily strengthening realisation that she was becoming more and more important to his happiness than he had ever allowed himself to believe before.

By the time they caught the flight home to Milan, on Friday afternoon, he knew he was almost ready to make the ultimate commitment. Only—

He wanted to see what Kranst had planned before he laid himself open. Antonia hadn't mentioned Kranst. *He* hadn't mentioned him. But had she been in touch with him? Did she know what Kranst was up to? Did she know that Marco was worrying about it? Did she care?

He needed to know the answers before he made any kind of commitment because, damn it, he had his pride to protect here!

It was a hesitation that was going to cost him, though Marco couldn't have any way of knowing it then.

They arrived back at the apartment late on Friday afternoon, to find Carlotta back at her post and smiling

her usual welcome. She thanked them for the postcards
Antonia must have sent her, then went on to relay a
series of messages, most of them business, but some
from his mother wanting him to call her as soon as he
got in.

'My father?' he questioned sharply.

But Carlotta shook her head. 'I asked,' she said.
'Your *mamma* assured me he was pleasingly well.'

So he nodded, and decided to leave any calls home
until after this evening was over.

That was another mistake.

There were also several calls for Antonia from Stefan
Kranst which, from their content, told him that Antonia
had held faith and not attempted to contact Kranst while
they'd been away. He wanted to wrap her in his arms
and kiss her for that, but good sense warned him not to
make an issue of it—just as she was sensibly asking no
questions about that other taboo subject, his parents.

Franco rang as they were sharing a pot of coffee
while relaxing for an hour in front of the TV before
they needed to start getting ready to go out. Marco felt
fine, very at peace with himself and the beautiful creature curled up beside him. He and Franco chatted as
best friends do. He was thanked for the painting they'd
given the de Maggios as an anniversary present, and for
the thought which had gone into it, and tried to pass the
whole thing off as if he knew exactly what Franco
meant. But he didn't, and his gaze was sardonic when
he remembered how easily he had let Antonia off without answering that little bone of contention between
them. Then he suggested dinner somewhere after the
Kranst showing.

It was at that moment that the tension began to creep
in. Antonia sat up and away from him. Studying her

profile, he heard Franco telling him that he and Nicola were not going tonight because they were spending the weekend up at Lake Como with her parents. Franco suggested Wednesday instead. Marco agreed, then hurriedly rang off.

'What's wrong?' he asked instantly.

'Nothing,' she replied. 'I think I'll go and get my shower now—'

But he wasn't so easily fooled. 'Kranst can only hurt you if you let him,' he said quietly.

'It isn't me Stefan hurts, Marco,' she replied, smiled a sad smile and walked away.

She was referring to him, of course, and it was a strange experience to acknowledge that she was right. Kranst did have the power to hurt him. He hurt Marco's pride and his ego, because the artist had a part of Antonia he had never been able to touch. What part that was exactly he had not been able to work out, but it had something to do with the way she refused to accept any hint of criticism where Kranst was concerned, whereas Marco she could find fault with very easily.

CHAPTER SIX

THE Romano Gallery claimed prestige position in the famous Quadrilatero. It was double-fronted in plate glass, with black steel framework, and Rosetta Romano's name made its point with eye-level modesty in black lettering on the door.

Class wasn't in it. Only people of substance dared place their fingers on that door. A black-suited lackey did it for Marco and Antonia, pulling it inwards with panache and a crisp, '*Buon giorno*, Signor Bellini—*signorina.*'

The interior was an artistic exhibit in its own right—white walls, white floor and a white stairway leading up to the main gallery rooms. Its only decoration was a single black spot, strategically placed on one wall to offer perspective.

Marco's hand at the base of her spine kept her moving towards the stairway. They took it together, climbing towards the two black-clothed waiters stationed at the top, holding trays loaded with glasses of champagne. Neither took a glass. To swallow right now would be an impossibility, with the tension rising steadily since they'd left the sitting room back at the apartment.

She had thought of ringing Stefan and insisting he explain about the painting so she could then decide whether to come or not. But two things had stopped her. One had something to do with a complicated thing called loyalty. To speak to Stefan just now seemed to be putting her loyalty to Marco into question. And the second was because she knew Marco would insist on coming here tonight no matter what she wanted to do. It was a male pride thing. Stefan had thrown him a challenge and Marco would rather slit his own throat than decline it.

But that didn't mean she hadn't spent time on her own, going over every painting from her days living with Stefan, looking for the one he had not shown in public before. As far as she could recall there wasn't one—which worried her all the more, because he had to have something up his sleeve or he wouldn't have thrown down that teasing gauntlet to Marco in the first place.

Dressed from neck to toe in black, at least she blended in with the status quo tonight, she then observed, as her gaze flicked around a semi-packed anteroom that fed into the main viewing rooms. Her hair was up, caught in a twist of black velvet, and her only adornment was a gold chain necklace with a single teardrop diamond that Marco had placed around her throat just before they left the apartment. The diamond nestled against the black of her dress and sparkled as she moved.

'Stunning,' Marco had called her. 'Too lovely to resist. Too perfect to touch.'

But she still didn't deserve his surname, she mused, with a mockery that was a long way from humorous.

'Ah, *buona sera*!' Rosetta Romano came to greet them with all the extravagance of an Italian hostess. 'Marco, *mi amore*…' Both elegant hands touched his face, then were replaced with kisses to both cheeks. 'Do you realise it must be over a year since you visited me here?'

It was a scold issued in the nicest possible way. While Marco said all the right things in reply Antonia studied Rosetta Romano, who had been a legend in her time for choosing husbands by the size of their wallets. Now that her beauty was fading she preferred to be known for her artistic eye. All the big names had exhibited here. Two years ago Stefan would not have stood a chance. Now—?

Rosetta turned her attention to Antonia. Her eyes sharpened, then narrowed searchingly. 'Yes.' She nodded. 'I see it. Stefan assured me I would. *Buona sera,* Signorina Carson,' she greeted with a slightly wry smile. 'It is a pleasure to meet you at last.'

Kisses on both cheeks were compulsory in Milan. The whisper Rosetta placed in her ear was most definitely not. 'Stefan is such a wicked man. I do hope you are prepared for this.'

No, she wasn't, and keeping that from showing on her face took a lot of self-control. But she wasn't able to stop the small anxious shiver from chasing down her spine. Marco felt it, and his hand moved on her waist to draw her closer to his side.

'What did she say to you?' he questioned when Rosetta floated away to greet her next arriving guests.

Antonia didn't even try to dress it up. 'She wanted to know if I was ready for whatever is coming,' she told him.

'And are you?' he asked curtly.

She flashed him a look. 'The point is, are you?' she coolly countered. 'Since you seem to believe that anything to do with me and Stefan is deliberately engineered to reflect badly on you.'

She was right and he knew it. A muscle flexed in his jaw. Then he was forced to offer an amiable smile to some friends who immediately accosted them. After that it was other friends. Progress towards their main objective became a laboriously slow affair. With his hand never leaving contact with her, Marco conversed lightly with acquaintances while Antonia stood beside him, eyes constantly looking around the steadily thickening crowd in search of Stefan. But still he hadn't put in an appearance.

What was he up to? Why was he piling on the tension like this?

People began filtering off into the adjoining rooms. With the smoothness of a man in no kind of hurry, Marco manoeuvred them into doing the same.

Antonia held her breath, Marco's hand pressed her just the bit closer to his side as they stepped through to the main gallery. Together they paused, together they took stock of what was presented—and together they began to frown.

For there was nothing on these walls that could warrant the challenge with which Stefan had lured them here—if you didn't count the evidence that Stefan had seemingly found himself a new subject to occupy his genius.

She was tall, she was dark, she was exquisitely different, and her rich African beauty could not have been further removed from what had gone before her. The long slender line of her body laid bare a sensuality that curled around the senses, the silken quality of her skin set fingers twitching with a need to reach out and touch. But, as usual, with Stefan, it was her eyes that drew you.

No hint of mirrors or ghosts anywhere, but a luxurious darkness that seemed to hold all the secrets of the universe.

Understanding came, trailing gentle fingertips over her emotions in the heart-rippling realisation that here, in these frames, was Stefan's salvation.

He had set himself free.

'Are you all right?' Marco asked gruffly.

'Yes,' she whispered. But he knew that she wasn't. He could feel her fighting a battle with tears as they walked from frame to frame. 'She's incredible, don't you think?'

'Bellisima,' Marco quietly agreed. And he knew he should be pleased by what he was seeing, but in truth he wanted to wring Kranst's selfish neck for choosing this way to tell her he had finally found someone else who drew this depth of emotion from him.

'I presume by your response that you knew nothing about her?'

'Not a thing,' she replied, having to swallow the tears again.

'Maybe you should ask him,' he suggested, and drew her attention to where Stefan Kranst was standing, not far away, watching her responses with an intensity that made Marco's blood boil.

Her head twisted round, her breath caught for a second, then her slender waist was sliding away from his hand. Without another word to him, she crossed the room towards a man who had always held too much power over her for Marco's peace of mind. Grimly he watched her pause a step away, watched her head tilt to one side as it tended to do when she asked a question. He saw Stefan Kranst's handsome face break into a rakish grin, and wanted to hit the self-obsessed bastard!

'Who is she?' was the question Antonia had put to Stefan.

'My saviour,' Stefan had grinned.

'Her name?' she demanded.

'Tanya,' he provided.

'Tanya...' Antonia repeated, and let her gaze drift to the nearest painting, where Tanya's smile held the rich knowledge of all men's needs. 'It suits her,' she murmured, then on a burst of soft laughter she went into his arms. 'Oh, I'm so happy for you!' she cried.

Across the room, Marco turned away from that embrace to continue to view the painting in front of him as if he had no problem at all with his woman falling into her ex-lover's arms once again. Someone sidled up beside him.

Of course it had to be Louisa. 'I do admire your confidence in those two, Marco,' she drawled lightly. 'Now, if, for argument's sake, *he* belonged to me, I would be over there scratching *her* eyes out by now.'

'But he doesn't belong to you—he belongs to her,' he said, indicating the beautiful black woman whose naked form exuded sexual contentment from every gifted brushstroke. 'And Antonia,' he then added very softly, 'belongs to me.'

With that he walked away, in no mood to play tit-for-tat word games tonight. He wanted his woman back, and he wanted her now!

'When do I meet her? Where is she?' Antonia was demanding of Stefan.

'Back in London, hiding away from you,' he drawled lazily. 'Just in case I was wrong about you, and you are secretly in love with me.'

Catching her soft burst of laughter as he approached, Marco also heard Antonia's amused reply. 'Of course you told her that I will always love you?'

'Hello, Marco,' Stefan greeted, a trifle drily. 'Come to claim Antonia?'

The man could read minds.

'We have to be leaving soon,' Marco answered smoothly. 'Another engagement, I'm afraid,' he invented with bland ease.

The moment he began speaking Antonia moved to his side and slipped her hand into the crook of his arm. She was making a point here, Marco recognised. And it should feel good.

So why did he feel as if she was taking second best by coming to him like this?

Irritation flicked to life. What the hell was he talking about? He scorned his own crazy imagination. He had never played second best to anyone in his life!

'Dare I ask the expert for an opinion?' Kranst reclaimed his attention. His expression was slightly wry, slightly challenging Marco to do his worst.

But Marco found he no longer wanted to play tit-for-tat games with Kranst, either. He just wanted to get Antonia somewhere private so he could make her forget Stefan Kranst's name!

So, 'You must know you've done it again,' he said easily. 'Have you sold the reproduction rights yet?'

'Still negotiating.' Stefan smiled. Then, 'Thank you, Marco,' he added seriously. 'Your opinion means a lot to me.'

And to your reputation, Marco added silently. Though anyone with eyes should be able to see that the man was about to make his second killing here.

Glancing down, he found Antonia was smiling up at him as if he had just bestowed the greatest accolade he possibly could. It made him want to shake her for still caring so much about Kranst's precious ego when it was clear the man didn't give a damn about hers!

'It's time we were leaving,' he told her, wishing they

hadn't bothered to come here at all. The man was a menace—to him and to Antonia!

'Before you do that,' Stefan Kranst inserted, looking at Antonia, 'I have something for you, my darling, if you remember...'

Beside him, Marco felt her stiffen. 'You mean this isn't surprise enough?' she laughed, in a voice strapped by strain.

'No.' The artist's smile was rueful. 'Special gifts come in solid form.'

Marco frowned at the answer, because it wasn't true. Not where Antonia was concerned. It was a lesson he had learned himself only last week via the red Lotus. Then he remembered Kranst's remark about the *Mirror Woman*, felt his own tension rise up to meet Antonia's, and realised that she had remembered a whole lot sooner than he had done.

'I have it waiting in Rosetta's office,' Stefan Kranst said smoothly, and turned away to stride purposefully towards Rosetta Romano's private office.

It really left them with no choice but to follow. 'This had better be worth the build-up,' Marco muttered, unable to stop himself.

'I hope not,' Antonia mumbled in reply, which just about said it all for both of them.

Rosetta Romano's office was a large white space of modern stylism. The only thing, therefore, that stood out in the room, was the giant black easel holding a large frame covered by a piece of fine black muslin.

The moment she saw it Antonia released a gasp of recognition, 'Stefan...no!' she shot out.

But Stefan was not willing to listen. He was already standing beside the easel and, with an agonising smoothness he trailed away the fine sheet covering.

Total silence arrived in starbursts of pain-bright recognition. Antonia began to tremble. Marco simply left her standing there and moved on legs suddenly in danger of collapsing to stand right in front of the painting.

It could have been a copy of the *Mirror Woman*. Certainly it was the same balcony, the same morning half-light touching that same sensual hint of gold to her silk-smooth skin. And it was certainly Antonia standing there naked, looking back over her shoulder in much the same way as the Mirror Woman did.

But it wasn't the same painting. For this was no mirror reflection, there was no emptiness in her beautiful eyes. Instead they were filled with the truth.

Antonia was held paralysed by exposure, static eyes fixed on Marco's hardening profile, static heart threatening to burst in her breast. She wanted to run, but she couldn't. She wanted to say something in her defence, but she couldn't do that because the evidence was so terribly damning.

Stefan came to stand beside her. His hand took hold of her hand and gave it a comforting squeeze. But she didn't feel comforted. Standing here watching the man she loved grimly coming to terms with the knowledge that she had been deceiving him filled her with the kind of dread that made every nerve-end she possessed scream in agony.

'I can't believe you've done this without my approval,' she managed to breathe out fraily.

'If I had asked, you wouldn't have given it,' Stefan gently replied.

'But *why* have you done it?' It seemed such a betrayal from the one person in this world she trusted completely.

'It was time he knew,' he said simply. 'You've let it

go on too long. You must know that by now, my darling.'

Knowing it and wanting *this* were two separate issues! 'You should not have done it,' she whispered, and felt her eyes start to burn as Marco reached out to touch the painting. A long finger gently grazed across a perfectly formed, blemish-free shoulder. Antonia felt that graze as if he'd reached out and touched her. Response shuddered through her on an electric spasm.

'I'll never forgive you,' she told Stefan, and stepped away from him with the intention of going to this other man who was so very important to her—

Only to freeze yet again, when Marco chose the same moment to turn.

His face looked as if it had been chiselled out of marble. 'You didn't paint this.' He honed his cold eyes directly on Stefan.

It was a clearly defined accusation. 'There speaks the voice of an expert,' Stefan smiled. Then, 'No,' he admitted. 'This was—'

'Mine,' Antonia put in unequivocally. 'It belongs to me!' She looked at Marco for understanding. 'It isn't even Stefan's to give to me! I *own* it! No one is supposed to—'

Marco's hard-eyed narrowed look silenced her. 'Who painted it?' he demanded.

'Does it matter?' she begged. 'It has never been put on public display and it never will be, Marco! I never—'

'I didn't ask if it had been shown,' he cut in. 'I asked you who the hell painted it!'

His fury was spectacular. Antonia drew back a step in dismay. 'I think you're missing the point, Marco,' Stefan put in quickly. 'I didn't show you this to—'

It happened so quickly that Stefan had no time to react to it. With a smoothness of movement that gave no indication whatsoever of what he was intending to do, Marco took two strides and, with a lightning move of his long lean body, he floored Stefan with a punch to his jaw.

With a grunt, Stefan landed in a sprawl in front of him. Antonia's cry as she lurched towards them filled his ears. 'Why did you do that!' she choked as she bent down beside Stefan.

'For messing with your life. For messing with *my* life!' he ground out violently, then just turned and strode out of the door.

Antonia watched him go with her heart in her eyes. On a groan, Stefan sat up and put a hand to his jaw. He was shaking his head as if he couldn't quite believe he had allowed that to happen.

'What have you done to me?' Antonia sobbed out.

'Fulfilled one of your dearest wishes and got him to punch my lights out,' Stefan very drily replied.

Not the least bit in the mood for his kind of dry humour, she came upright then bent to help him get up. 'Has he hurt you?' she asked.

'Don't sound so sympathetic.' He mocked her frosty enquiry. 'Split my lip, that's all,' he then answered, only to really infuriate her by suddenly beginning to laugh!

'Stop it!' she choked. 'How dare you laugh at a time like this? What have you *done* to me, Stefan? *Why* have you done it?' The tears began to swim as she stared at the closed office door. 'He's never going to forgive me for this. You do know that,' she told him thickly. 'He's even left without me!'

'Not that man,' Stefan stated confidently. 'Give me a minute to put some ice on this, and we'll go out there and find him. I promise you,' he assured her pained white expression, 'he's going to be there...'

But Marco didn't want to be found for, having walked out on one ugly scene, he now found himself standing outside Rosetta Romano's door, flexing his abused fist and staring directly at the looming threat of yet another scene.

His mother had arrived. God alone knew where she had come from—and God alone knew why, when he'd believed her safely ensconced in Tuscany. But there she was, holding court in the middle of the ante-room surrounded by a host of delighted old friends and acquaintances.

In the black mood he was in, he actually contemplated pretending he hadn't seen her and getting the hell out of there before she saw him!

Only he was not leaving without Antonia, he determined, with a grimness that promised a glimpse at hell for someone. And it took only a thin sliver of common sense to get through his anger, to tell him that he couldn't avoid speaking to his own mother, for goodness' sake!

But a meeting between her and Antonia? His blood ran cold at the very idea of it. It was a sensation that forced him to work hard at pulling a smooth mask down on his bubbling anger and then striking out towards his mother with the grim intention of getting the mother-son reunion out of the way *before* Antonia decided to put in an appearance with her famous ex-lover in tow!

But lady luck was not working in Marco's favour tonight. The room was pretty crowded with Milan's best. People who more or less knew each other on first-name terms. Isabella Bellini was known and liked by many. Her son even found an amused smile as he approached and saw just how many people were gathered around her slender form.

She saw him coming, and her lovely face broke into a welcoming smile. His smile became a rakish grin as he took this beautiful, delicate creature he adored into his arms and let her shower kisses all over his face.

Hands replaced kisses, followed by remarks to the crowd on how handsome he was, how cruel he was to his mother for not returning her calls. It was the Italian way. He accepted it and even enjoyed it. His apologies were profuse, his enquiries about his father sincere.

'He is having a good week,' his mother informed him—and the smiling circle. 'So he threw me out and told me not to come back for at least two days. He says I fuss too much, but in truth,' she confided, 'he plans to play cards, drink wine and gamble with his friends without me around to disapprove.'

The laughter was warm and appreciative. From the corner of his eye Marco saw the door to Rosetta Romano's office open; his skin began to prickle.

Isabella looked back at her son. 'And this one,' she announced, 'cannot even find the time in his busy life to answer his mother when she calls to him! I get his housekeeper,' she informed her audience.

Antonia was approaching him from his right. She looked pale, she looked anxious. She had no idea what she was going to walk into.

'I get the message service,' his mother was continuing. 'I have to ring his friends to discover where he might be this evening!' Marco smiled the expected rueful smile, and wondered which friend it was who had dropped him in this mess.

Antonia had now come to within a few paces of his right. Beside her was Stefan Kranst, wearing a bruise on his lip and a crooked smile. It was decision time, Marco accepted heavily. He either drew Antonia towards him, introduced her to his mother and risked offending his mother's outdated ideas on what was acceptable in polite society, or he ignored Antonia standing there and offended her. It was a lousy choice to have to decide.

Someone arrived at his left side, diverting his mother's attention. Her face broke into a beatific smile. 'Ah, Louisa,' she greeted. 'There you are! And looking so beautiful, as always. I was just telling everyone how I had to call you up to discover where my own son would be tonight...'

Louisa. It had to be Louisa, Marco noted grimly. The knowledge tipped the balance of his decision away from his mother. For no one had the right to try manipulating either him or his life, and maybe it was about time that his mother and Louisa realised that!

Louisa was being welcomed with the usual kisses from his mother when Marco turned the half-inch it required to catch Antonia's gaze. He saw the uncertainty there, the knowledge that she had recognised whom it was holding centre stage. His heart turned over. She was so beautiful. So much his woman, no matter what secrets she had been keeping from him, that it was suddenly no decision at all to smile and hold out his arm in invitation for her to come to him.

Her relief shone like the diamond at her lovely throat as she took the final irrevocable step which brought her beneath the protection of his arm and into the smiling circle.

Slender-boned, exquisitely turned out in matt-black crêpe, her satin-black hair sleek to her beautiful head, Isabella Bellini was just emerging from her embrace

with Louisa when she observed this little interplay—
and her eyes began to cool.

'Mother,' Marco said formally. 'I would like you to
meet—'

As if he hadn't spoken, and Antonia wasn't there,
Isabella Bellini simply turned her back on them. The
deadening silence that followed was profound.

It was such a blatantly deliberate act, that it was all
Antonia could do to remain standing there, with her
stinging eyes lowered, hiding the deep gouge of humiliation that was tearing into the very fabric her pride was
made of.

While Marco emulated a pillar of stone.

How many people actually witnessed what had just
happened, Antonia didn't know. But it really didn't take
an audience for her to understand that the cuckoo had
just been devastatingly exposed.

The hum of conversation suddenly rushed into over-
drive as people attempted to cover up the dreadful moment. Someone gently touched her arm. It was Stefan.
'That—' he growled, 'was unforgivable.'

She began to shake. Stefan glanced angrily at Marco,
who still hadn't moved a single muscle. Then, 'Come
on,' he murmured gruffly. 'Let's go back to
Rosetta's—'

'No,' a hard voice countermanded. And with it Marco
broke free from his stone-like stasis. 'We are leaving,'
he announced.

The hand tightened on her shoulder. Antonia could
feel the anger in its biting grip and clenched the muscles
beneath it.

'I'm coming with you,' Stefan declared, still gripping
Antonia's arm. 'I have no wish to—'

'No.' Once again Marco cut him short. 'We appreciate your concern, but this is not your problem.'

'It is when it's Antonia who has been insulted,' Stefan said angrily.

'And *my* mother who did the insulting,' Marco coldly pointed out.

'Excuse me,' Antonia whispered, and broke free from both of them. She needed to get away from here, and she needed to do it now. Fighting tears, fighting the crawling worms of humiliation, fighting to keep her head up high as she went, she walked quickly for the stairs.

If she'd cared to look back, she would have seen that Marco's mother was already feeling the discomfort of what she had done. She was touching her son's arm, trying to get his attention. But Marco didn't even offer her a glance as he strode after Antonia. His hand found her waist and clamped her close. Together they started down the stairs. In her haste Antonia tripped over her own spindly shoes. Marco grimly held her upright, and kept her moving while the throb of his anger pulsed all around her like the heartbeat pound of a drum.

They reached the plate-glass door at the same time as the doorman pulled it open. Neither realised the door was being opened to allow someone outside to come in. There was a bump of bodies.

'*Scuze signor—signorina,*' a deep, quietly modulated voice apologised.

It was automatic to glance up. Automatic to attempt the polite reply to the apology. Antonia looked into the stranger's face, he looked into hers, and any attempt to speak was thoroughly suffocated beneath yet another thick layer of appalled dismay.

Black hair spiked with silver, grey eyes with a hint

of green. As tall as Marco, but more slender than Marco, he was a man in the autumn years of his life.

Still, she knew exactly who it was she was staring at—and, worse, he knew that she knew.

'*Madonna mia,*' he breathed in shaken consternation. 'Anastasia.'

Anastasia… It was too much in one short evening for Antonia to deal with. It was all she could do to shrink back into the only solid thing she could rely on right now.

Marco might be immersed in the red tide of anger, but he saw the exchanged looks, heard the name shudder from the other man's lips. Knew there was yet something else going on here that he wasn't privy to, and felt his anger switch from his mother and back to the woman now shrinking into his side.

'You are mistaken,' he clipped at the other man. 'Please excuse us,' he added coldly, then got them the hell out of there before anything else smashed into them.

Outside, the Quadrilatero was busy with window-shoppers. Marco's car was parked in a side street not far away. Holding on to his temper until he got them there was a case of clamping his mouth shut and saying nothing.

Opening the passenger door, he helped her into the plush black leather seat, then squatted down to lock home her seat belt. She didn't seem to notice. With yet another lash of anger, he grabbed her chin and made her look at him. Her eyes were almost black, her skin paste-white and her lovely mouth completely bloodless. She looked as fragile as a piece of fine Venetian glass, likely to shatter without careful handling.

But he didn't feel like handling anything carefully.

In fact, he wanted to shatter her into little pieces so he could reach the real woman, because this one had become a complete stranger to him!

With a harsh sigh he released her chin, stood up and closed the car door. He got in beside her, then fired the engine. Jaw locked, teeth clenched, he set them moving, bullying his way into the nose-to-tail traffic clogging up Milan's crazy one-way road system, then took an amount of pleasure in doing the same thing in his quest to forge them the most direct route home.

Car horns blared at him in protest. Headlights flashed. Abuse was thrown at him in colourful Italian. He didn't care. He was so angry! Angry with Kranst and his little party piece. With his mother and her unforgivable behaviour! And he was angry with Antonia for allowing him to believe the painting he had in his apartment was of her!

And then there was the man in the gallery doorway, he added to his long list of grievances because, despite appearing otherwise, he'd recognised him. His name was Anton Gabrielli, a wealthy industrialist turned recluse, who had rarely been seen in public since his wife died several years ago.

And he might have called Antonia *Anastasia*, but the error had been irrelevant. He *knew* her! And, more to the point, Antonia had recognised him!

'How do you know Anton Gabrielli?' he demanded.

It was like talking to a puppet. 'I've never met him before in my life,' she answered woodenly.

'Don't lie to me!' he rasped. 'He may have got your name wrong, but you knew each other all right. The mutual horror was all too revealing.'

'I said I've never met him before!' she shouted. It was so out of character that he threw a sharp look at her. No puppet now, he noted. She was shaking so badly that it made the diamond at her throat shimmer. On a choked little gasp, she turned her face right away from him so he couldn't read it. It was the act of someone caught in a lie.

Without another word, he turned his attention to getting through the traffic, while a new filthy suspicion began to tear into him. Anton Gabrielli was about the same age as Kranst. If she'd enjoyed Kranst as a lover then why not Gabrielli? After all, what did he actually know about Antonia's life before Kranst?

Nothing, he realised. Absolutely nothing.

As the ugly green stuff began to replace his blood again, he finally managed to reach his goal and pulled them to a screeching stop in the basement car park of his apartment. He switched off the engine—then clamped a hard hand on Antonia's thigh as she released her seat belt.

'Stay,' he gritted. It was a dire warning. She wasn't going to make him kick his heels down here for a second time while she rode the lift alone.

The fingers fluttered, then went to rest on her lap, her body melting back into the seat. With a tight hiss of satisfaction he got out, swung round the car, opened her door then bent to help her alight.

The lift took them upwards, with her shaking like crazy and him with his fists clenched to stop him taking hold of her and shaking her some more! When they reached the apartment door it was Marco who opened it; Antonia didn't seem capable. But, once inside, the few seconds it required for him to deactivate the alarm system gave her the chance to get away from him.

She headed straight for the bedroom. He stayed where he was long enough to utter a few choice curses before grimly striding after her. If she'd locked the bedroom door on him then she was in for one hell of a shock! he vowed.

But the door wasn't locked. And what he found when he tossed it back on its hinges stunned him to a complete standstill.

CHAPTER SEVEN

'—WHAT the hell are you doing?' he raked out incredulously.

But he could see what she was doing. A suitcase already lay open on the bed and she was tossing things into it like a criminal on the run.

'Antonia!' he demanded when she didn't answer.

'I'm l-leaving,' she stammered, then froze within the midst of what he realised was full-scale panic to stand with body stiff, arms straight, fists tightly clenched, while she fought a battle with whatever emotion was suddenly trying to overwhelm her.

'The hell you are,' he grimly countered, but his own voice no longer sounded quite so steady.

He began striding towards her, and the act jolted her back from wherever she'd gone to and she turned on him, paste-white, stark-eyed—he had never seen an expression like it in all his life.

'*Cara…*' he murmured hoarsely. 'For goodness' sake…'

'I'm leaving you, Marco!' She almost screamed the words at him she was so out of control. 'Now—tonight! I n-never want to see you again.'

The fact that he could see it had almost killed her to say that didn't make him feel any better, because he could see she actually meant it—and that was scaring the life out of him.

She turned back to the suitcase. With a swipe of his hand he sent it flying to the floor. Clothes scattered everywhere. Silly things like a couple of sets of under-wear, a couple of skirts, a couple of simple cotton tops.

He tried swallowing and found he couldn't. He tried making sense of the evidence he was looking at. He couldn't do that either. For no woman—*no woman*! left Marco Bellini with only the clothes she'd come to him with!

No woman left Marco Bellini.

'You aren't going anywhere until you've answered some questions,' he growled, and grabbed her hand. 'Maybe once you've done that I'll be glad to see the back of you!' he threw in for furious good measure, and began trailing her behind him out of the bedroom and down the hall while she tried her best to get free of him.

No chance, he vowed silently. No damn chance.

Throwing open the door to his study, he strode them over to the locked door. Still holding her hand prisoner, he stabbed in the security pin-number, hauled her in-side, then over to the *Mirror Woman.*

'Now, let's start right here,' he gritted. 'Who is *she*?'

Anastasia, Antonia thought tragically, and began shaking all over again, fighting a battle with tears that reached right down to her abdomen. Sad, tragic—beau-tiful Anastasia.

'Mirror—mirror,' she whispered thickly.

'What is that supposed to mean?' Marco said harshly.

It was no use lying, no use trying to pretend that she didn't know what he was talking about. The game was up. She had been exposed as the fraud she was.

'This,' she said, 'is Anastasia…'

It took a few moments, then it hit him. 'My God,' he rasped. 'Are you saying that she is your twin?'

A laugh left her throat on a strangled sob. Her amber eyes shimmered with tears and a pained kind of hu-

mour, because Anastasia would have *so* loved to have
been here to hear this big handsome Italian say that.

'No, not my twin,' she murmured softly. 'She was
my mother...'

My poor, wretched, haunted mother, she silently extended, while the silence grew thick all around her.

'Mother,' Marco repeated, as if he had to do so to
understand the concept. 'You mean, you and Kranst actually....'

The words stopped. Antonia turned to look at him.
For once he was literally floundering on the rocks of
shock. And he looked white. He looked horrified.

'What?' she snapped as anger began flooding up from
the depths of a bitter knowledge of where they were
about to go with this. 'Did we collaborate to deceive
everyone? Yes.' She openly admitted the charge. 'Did
I pose nude for Stefan so he could pretend I was my
mother? No, I did not,' she denied that. 'Stefan and my
mother were lovers for ten years! He adored her. And
no *again*, before the cogs inside your head start turning
to something nasty,' she sliced at him. 'Stefan did *not*
bed-swap between my mother and myself!'

'I was not about to assume—' Marco began stiffly.

But angrily she cut in. 'You've *always* assumed!' she
cried. 'From the very beginning you assumed we were
lovers. But Stefan is my *friend*!' she threw at him. 'My
dear, dear friend who arrived in our lives when we really needed someone warm and loving and endlessly
giving like him! Between us, we nursed my mother
through a long and miserable illness. And the result of
those dark years?' She gestured with a trembling hand
towards the painting. 'How my mother *wanted* Stefan
to remember her. Not the withered and worn-out shell
she became towards the end!'

Tears flooded her eyes. She looked away from him, her whole torso heaving with the fight for control.

'So he painted a lie,' Marco said grimly.

'And what if he did?' she replied. 'What does it matter to anyone else that the image they see isn't the gruesome reality?'

'Hence the mirror.' Oh, he was very good, she had to give him that.

'It reflects what was,' she confirmed. 'Stefan could pick up a paintbrush even now and paint her looking exactly like this. He loved her so very much...'

'Yet he was quick to sell these when opportunity knocked,' Marco pointed out cynically. 'And he was quick to let you masquerade as her to add a bit of juicy notoriety to the sales!'

'I didn't say he was perfect,' she snapped. 'And the paintings went on show *before* my mother died!' she pronounced. 'At *her* request! For *her* pleasure! It *amused* her when people mistook me for her! And *anything* that made her happy, Stefan and I gave her!' Her eyes flashed, tear-bright but unrepentant.

His hardened into bitterness. 'That's all fine for everyone else. But don't you think you owed it to me to tell me the truth?'

'Why should I have done that?' she gasped out in angry bewilderment. 'You got what you came looking for, Marco,' she told him. 'You got the woman in the painting. You had no interest in me as a living breathing human being!'

Two streaks of colour hit his cheekbones, his whole body stiffened in affront. 'That's not true,' he denied.

'Yes, it is,' she insisted. 'Take away the kudos in being able to lay claim to Stefan Kranst's notoriously sexy model, and it would take away the desire; I always knew that.'

He didn't answer. For her, his silence said it all. Looking back at her mother for one last time, Antonia touched a gentle finger to the tiny birthmark on her shoulder, smiled a sad 'I love you' smile, then withdrew again, curling her fingers into her palms as she turned for the door.

'Where are you going?'

She paused, but didn't look back. 'Home,' she whispered. 'I'm going home. There's nothing left for me here.'

'I'm here,' Marco murmured gruffly.

'No, you're not.' Antonia shook her head. 'You're standing aloft in a place I can never reach you. It's called the social ladder. You don't mind coming down to the bottom rung to enjoy life with the masses now and then, but when it comes to elevating someone up to your top rung—no chance.' She laughed. It was a bitter sound. 'Élite marries élite. Darling Mamma expects it.'

'Leave my mother out of this,' he rasped back angrily.

'But why should I?' she spun round to demand. He looked so grim and remote it was almost as if he was already climbing back up that ladder and away from her. 'In truth,' she said, 'I'm actually grateful for what your mother did tonight. Because she forced me to take a good look and see just how I had been wasting my life living here with you.'

'Wasting it because I haven't asked you to marry me?' he threw back with contempt. 'Is that what your year-long investment in me has really been about, *cara*? Give a man what you think he wants. Lie to him, cheat him if necessary, in the wild hope that the dividend will give back the jackpot billionaire with all the luxury trimmings?'

He saw himself as the *jackpot*? 'You arrogant bastard,' she said scornfully. 'I invested in *love*!' she cried. 'As in my love for you being strong enough to ignite some love back by return! But it never happened, did it, Marco?' Her eyes began to shine like the diamond at her throat. 'And even after a whole year of living together you can still freeze up in dismay when confronted with the disapproval of your mother, *and still stand here* and toss your contempt at me for actually daring to think myself fit to marry you!'

'I did *not* freeze in shame because of *you*!' he raked back angrily. 'I froze in shame of my wretched mother!'

But he was shouting it to an empty space. Antonia had already walked away. For all of five seconds he remained where he was, wanting to just let her go and stew in her own dignity. But then he remembered the suitcase on the floor of the bedroom and calculated how quickly it would take her to repack it.

Anger shot through him. Curses rattled from his tense lips. But alarm set his feet moving. He hated it—*hated feeling like this*!

Sure enough she was in the bedroom, standing over the bloody case. 'All right!' he lashed out. 'Marry me! If that is what it takes to stop this—craziness. Marry me—*marry me!*'

She turned to look at him. It was like watching snow cover a mountain her skin turned so white. Then the rain came, flooding into those beautiful amber eyes and her lips erupted with an agonised quiver.

Shaken to the roots by his own proposal, stunned beyond movement by her response, he watched one of

her hands come out and give a flick in a bitter throw
away gesture. Then she began walking towards him. His
skin came alive to a million bee-stings; his heart lost
the ability to beat. When she reached him she paused,
and those awful tear-washed eyes looked right into his.

'May you go to hell, Marco,' she whispered thickly,
then pushed him out of the way so that she could get
past him.

It took him several moments to gain the will to move
again. By then, a door further down the hallway had
shut and the key had been turned. Staring round the
chaos she had left behind her, he suddenly felt like a
man standing in the middle of a ruin. Helpless, hope-
less, unable to come to terms with how quickly it had
all come tumbling down around him.

His legs eventually managed to take him forward, his
feet picking their way through the debris of her clothes.
Sitting down on the bed, he leant forward and clasped
his head between long tense fingers.

He could have played an old scene again and gone
charging after her, but it didn't even come up as an
option this time. She needed to cool off, and he needed
to get a grip on what had just happened because at this
precise moment he didn't have a single clue!

One minute he had been the one with all the grievances; the next Antonia had been spilling hers out all
over him. His sigh was heavy, shot with a residue of
anger and frustration because so much of what she had
thrown at him was true!

Her mother…he remembered, and got up with a
swing of his body that responded to a sudden clutch of
dismay. His feet took him back to his study, took him
back to the *Mirror Woman* where he stood gazing into
a face he'd believed he knew. But the differences were

already manifesting themselves, as if someone had come along and altered certain brushstrokes. The curve of her eyebrows, the tilt of her jaw, the way her slender neck blended into her slender shoulders. The birthmark he'd assumed was the artist's carelessness with his paintbrush. All very subtle differences that only an expert eye would ever notice.

He'd thought he had that expert eye. He'd believed he was a great connoisseur, when in actual fact Antonia was right and he was merely one of many, seeing only what he wanted to see.

Now he could look at this sad creature and pick out a hundred differences between her and her beautiful daughter—if he could bring himself to look at the rest of her, that was. It felt like a sin to do so now. He'd always thought Kranst the voyeur in this painting, and it didn't sit comfortably to realise that the real voyeur had been himself.

It made him want to turn the darn thing to the wall and forget he'd ever seen it. But—

This was Antonia's *mother*, he reiterated bleakly. Antonia loved this woman. It had been there in every word that she spoke! To turn her to the wall would be a rejection of someone who was as precious to Antonia as his own mother was to him.

Though he didn't want to think about his own mother right now, he accepted with an angry hardening of his jaw.

And Antonia had never been uncomfortable with the nudity in this painting. Her discomfort had been in looking at someone she had loved and lost, not the nudity itself.

Not her own nudity—or her mother's, he extended, as many things began to make sense. She had lived for ten years with an artist who specialised in the naked female form. He had a gift—no, a genius—for the genre, therefore it was only natural that she would learn to see nudity as something to appreciate in its own right, and not something to turn away from in shame. As it had been to him until he discovered who it was he was actually looking at!

Since when had he developed a bigot's view of something this special? Marco asked himself. This was art! Master-class art! If he'd been in a better frame of mind, he would have been purchasing one of Kranst's latest offerings. And not just for the investment, but because he *liked* what Kranst painted on the canvas!

But *who* had painted Antonia's nude image? he then asked himself, and felt his whole sophisticated outlook tumble like a house of cards. Anger enveloped him, spewing forth from a strange place inside him that could now accept Kranst as her painter—but not some other man!

How the heck had she managed to divert him so thoroughly that he hadn't demanded some answers about him? And there was Anton Gabrielli lurking in the shadows.

Behind Marco the telephone started ringing. If it did nothing else it diverted his attention away from what was beginning to flood his veins again.

He walked over to his desk and stood there making no attempt to pick up the receiver. His mother? he wondered. Wanting to voice her disapproval in more detail? Kranst, wanting to know if Antonia was still alive?

He let his answering service take over. By the time it had silenced the telephone ring he had closed the door on the study. He didn't want to talk to anyone, and he certainly didn't want to listen to them prose all over him.

What he wanted was Antonia. But not yet, he grimly reiterated. And not at all tonight, until all of these ugly feelings rattling around inside him had been given a chance to calm down.

Antonia's insides were shaking, the fight to hold back the tears strangling the ability to breathe. Without really knowing what she was doing, she walked over to the bed and began tugging at the back zip to her dress as if it was perfectly natural to undress—when in actual fact she should be getting away from here. Not hiding behind a locked door which only extended the agony!

The zip snagged between her shoulderblades. She struggled with it for a while, with her head lowered and her eyes concentrated on the diamond at her throat. The zip wouldn't budge. It seemed a kind of justice, after the night she had just had, that it should do so at a point where she had no hope of wriggling out of the dress. On a trembling sigh of frustration she diverted her fingers to the necklace, removed it, then just stood there staring at nothing.

Had he really had the gall to offer to marry her, then stand there looking as if he'd just committed a mortal sin?

'Oh.' She choked on a tear that managed to escape. I should hate him. I should hate him for saying it the way he did, she told herself. But it wasn't hate she was feeling, it was hurt, because he hadn't meant it. He had merely been determined to grab the higher ground in an argument which made little sense to begin with! What a dreadful night, she sighed out bleakly. What a terrible, eye-opening, miserable night.

Beginning with Stefan springing that painting on them without warning. Then moving on to Marco's mother's neat little snub that was still managing to crease her up with pained mortification.

And, if all of that wasn't enough, she had to come face to face with Anton Gabrielli. A shiver ripped through her as something hard and cold turned pain to anger. How he dared to even whisper her mother's name after what he had done to her, she would never know!

But to do it in front of Marco of all people, was the ultimate sin she would never forgive Gabrielli for. *He* had been the final ruin of everything. *He* was the reason she had to leave here or risk the kind of scandal Marco would never forgive her for.

Did Anton Gabrielli know? Had he guessed by now that he had just come face to face with his daughter?

Then—no. She denied that. She was *not* his daughter. His was merely the seed which had formed the base of her conception. She'd never known him, never met him and didn't want to. In fact, she would rather remain the notorious Mirror Woman than lay claim to a father who had deserted her mother as soon as he'd known she was pregnant.

And what immortal words had he used to do it? 'Men like me don't marry their mistresses. It is not your function.'

God, she hated him.

Therefore she should hate Marco too, since he had used similar words to her not that long ago. What would his mother say if she knew about Anton Gabrielli? 'The sins of the mother,' would be oh, so appropriate. The same looks, the same paintings, the same attraction to tall dark handsome Italian billionaires!

Bitterness welled. Tears still cut her throat in two.

She turned for the door with the intention of keeping to her original decision and just getting away from here!

Yet when she reached the door she just couldn't do it! Oh, what was to become of her if she couldn't even bring herself to walk away now, when there was nothing left for her here? Nothing!

'I'm here,' Marco had said to her.

Wrapping her arms around her body, she hugged that gruffly spoken statement to her for all she was worth as her restless feet took her the other way, over to the huge floor-to-ceiling windows which gave access out onto the terrace.

Sliding one of them open, she stepped outside in the vague hopes that some fresh air would clear her confusion. But it was stifling out here after the air-conditioned interior. Still, rather than go back inside, she moved over to one of the sun loungers, slipped out of her shoes, sat down and curled her knees up so she could rest her chin on them.

The terrace was a very impressive part of the apartment, which wrapped round two full sides of the building. When Marco threw one of his extravagant parties all the doors would be opened so every room leading in from the terrace could be used for one function or another. And the sound of music and life and laughter would follow you everywhere.

But tonight it was more silent than she'd ever known it. Even Milan's constant traffic way down below her seemed to have stopped running.

Or maybe it's me who's stopped, Antonia mused bleakly. The way fate had come along and hit her with just about everything tonight, it could be its way of making her stand still and face reality.

But she didn't want reality, she thought with a sigh that sent her brow onto her knees. She wanted things back the way they used to be—lies, uncertainties and all…

CHAPTER EIGHT

IT WAS around two o'clock in the morning when Marco
slid open the door to the terrace and stepped outside.
Behind him lay the rumpled bed he had just given up
on. He couldn't sleep. The bed felt strange without
Antonia sharing it with him. So he'd pulled on a thin
black robe and gone to the kitchen to raid the fridge
before deciding to come out here to eat his sandwich,
drink a glass of soothing red wine—and brood.

Making for one of the loungers, he adjusted the back-
rest into its upright position, sat down, then stretched
out his long legs with an accompanying sigh.

It was a hot humid night, but anything was preferable
to that bed without Antonia in it with him. In fact, he
might just spend the rest of the night out here.

It was either this or he convinced Antonia to open
her door for him. And since he'd lasted this long without giving in to that particular urge, he could last until
dawn, he told himself, and made his shoulders more
comfortable against the cushions, took a sip at the wine,
then closed his eyes.

It was peaceful, he noticed. Pleasant, if you didn't
count the heat. And the darkness was acting like a
shroud, holding at bay all of those things he didn't want
to think about.

Shame a soft sound had to disturb him. In fact he
would have ignored it if there hadn't been something
very familiar about it, like one of those sensual soft

119

sighs Antonia had a habit of making when she was sleeping.

Opening his eyes again, he turned his head.

She was less than ten feet away, lying on her side with her back towards him. If it hadn't been for the oatmeal colour of the lounger cushions he wouldn't have seen her through the darkness, but the black dress outlined her slender shape.

The muscles around his heart contracted, knocking its even rhythm onto a different beat. Getting up, he put the plate and the wineglass down on a nearby table then began walking towards her with the silence of bare feet. Rounding the end of the lounger, he stood for a moment gazing down at her. There was a painfully vulnerable look about the way she was lying on her side, with her arms crossed over her breasts and her head turned downwards so her hair covered her lovely face.

Squatting down beside her, he gently lifted her hair up and brushed the silken spirals over her shoulder. The first thing he noticed was how hot she felt to the touch; the next was the evidence of tears on her cheeks.

His heart pulled a different trick by actually hurting. He didn't like to think she had been alone out here crying. He didn't like to know that she had probably been crying because of him.

She must have sensed his presence because her eye-lashes fluttered, her soft mouth parted on another one of those sighs. Then her eyelids lifted to reveal sleep-darkened beautiful eyes—and she smiled at him.

When had she ever opened her eyes and *not* smiled at him like this? Marco asked himself painfully. And those eyes were awash with love for him. Always love. *Why* did he find it so impossible to return the words? Because he felt the emotion—*Dio*, he felt it. In fact he had been feeling it for ever, only he'd refused to acknowledge it to himself.

A set of slender white fingers came up to touch his cheek. They moved to his eyebrows then dropped to run the length of his half-smiling mouth. For a man who had been used since birth to having his face lovingly touched like this, this was touching like no other touching he had ever experienced. It was like being anointed with the sweetest blessing ever.

Lifting his hand to capture those fingers, he made his own loving gesture by pressing a kiss to her palm. Her eyes flooded with warmth and his began to gleam. They had always been able to make love with the smallest of intimacies. It was what made their relationship so special.

'Hi,' he murmured softly. 'What are you doing sleeping out here?'

It was then that she realised where she was—and, more to the point, *why* she was out here. The hand was withdrawn, along with the smile and the love. Looking away from him, she slid her feet to the floor so she could sit up. It was his cue to stand up and give her some space, but he was damned if he was going to withdraw now he had her within touching distance. So he remained squatting there in front of her while she made a thing of finger-combing her hair and trying, he supposed, to regroup her defences.

'What time is it?' she asked.

Irritation sparked to life. What did it matter what time it was? 'You didn't answer my question,' he prompted.

'The zip caught on my dress,' she replied, as if that should explain everything.

But it didn't. 'And you couldn't come to me for help with it?'

Of course she couldn't, and her expression told him that. On a sigh he stood upright. So did she, then went to move around him, but he stopped her with a hand on her shoulder.

'Don't go, *cara*,' he said. 'At least not until you have asked me what *I* am doing out here.'

The prompt made her hesitate. She glanced up at him warily. He smiled a wryly self-mocking smile. 'The bed was too empty without you in it beside me,' he confessed. He felt the tension easing out of her shoulder and added huskily, 'Come back there with me?'

She wanted to. He saw it written in her eyes before she lowered them again with a small shake of her head. 'I don't think it would be a good idea,' she murmured.

'Because we argued?' he said. 'We always argue. It is a part of who we are.'

But this was different. He knew it was different. And by the shake of her hair, Antonia did too. 'Too much has happened...'

'Nothing we cannot work out, *cara mia*,' he gently certified. And if she shook her head again, he swore he would use other methods to persuade her!

She didn't shake her head. 'I don't want to talk about it—'

'I never mentioned talking,' he murmured drily.

Her eyes came back to his. 'I don't want to do *that* either,' she flashed.

That assumption earned her a lazy grin—until he felt her begin to tense up again. 'Sleep,' he offered. 'Where we both prefer to be. In our bed, curled around each other. Nothing more, nothing less. What do you say, *cara*, hmm?'

What did she say? Antonia asked herself wistfully. She said *yes* to him because she had never been able to say *no*. And she was tired and miserable, so she might as well be miserable curled up against him than miserable out here on her own, she justified her weakness.

So with a small nod of her head she gave him his answer. His arm came about her shoulders. It felt so good to feel it there that she released a sigh, gave in and leaned closer. They didn't speak again as they walked the terrace towards their bedroom. Marco was keeping silent because he had got what he wanted and didn't want to chance spoiling it. Antonia was silent because she knew she should not be letting him this close again, yet couldn't bring herself to turn away.

He was her weakness. He always would be.

The first thing she noticed when they stepped through the open window was the room had been swept clean of her clothes and suitcase. The next was the rumpled bed, which told its own story.

Still maintaining the silence which this short truce had been built upon, when they reached the bed Marco turned her so he could deal with the snagged zipper on her dress. Her hair was in the way. She reached up to gather the silken tresses over one shoulder. It was as dark in the bedroom as it had been out on the terrace. The dress was black, the zipper was black, so it took a little while for him to untangle the teeth from the snagged piece of fabric. By the time he sent the zip sliding free Marco had a feeling Antonia had stopped breathing. And the first moment she could she stepped away from him, to remove the dress herself.

He grimaced, and contained the urge to finish a job he had always found a pleasure. Instead he turned his attention to straightening out the crumpled evidence of his restless hours alone in here. When he turned back to her again the dress had gone, to reveal black silk underwear that did wonderful things to her pale skin. And, though he couldn't be sure in the darkness, he had a suspicion she was blushing, which made him frown, because he could not remember a time that she'd ever been shy in front of him, other than the first time they'd made love. And then, if he hadn't known better, he'd have sworn he'd been her first ever lover.

But there was worse to come when she actually tried to get into the bed without removing anything else. The fault of those paintings? His mother? Or was it *his* fault that she wanted to hide what she had always been so comfortable with?

'No,' he said. Then, 'No,' again, with a completely different meaning placed in the word. The first had been a protest, the second a plea.

When she hesitated, he used the moment to step behind her and unfasten her bra strap. Black silk fell away from pale satin flesh, her beautiful breasts were set free. She removed the rest herself without comment then slipped between the sheets—all without once letting him see her face.

Grimly he stripped off his robe and joined her. In silence he drew her into the curve of his body. She settled as she always did, but he could feel the guard she had placed on herself that was stopping her from melting against him.

The urge to say something got the better of him, even at the risk of causing yet another scene. 'I don't like to fight with you,' he admitted as he nuzzled his lips into the scented flow of her hair.

'I know,' she replied. And she did, he realised. He found it rather disturbing to have to admit that she knew him a whole lot better than he actually knew her. 'But this changes nothing, Marco,' she obviously felt compelled to add.

Was she talking about leaving him? On that dark thought, one of his hands found her breast, one of his legs hooked over hers to keep her close, with the curve of her lower body nestling into the cradle of his hips. 'Go to sleep,' he said on a heavy sigh, while willing himself not to challenge that final statement and just take his own advice and go to sleep.

It was a crazy idea. You didn't sleep when you'd both been through the emotional mill as they had tonight. You didn't sleep when it was all still churning round in your head.

And you didn't sleep when the woman in your arms was implying that she intended to leave you.

What you did was move closer to that same woman. You let your hand increase its pressure on what it was holding. You buried your face in the sweet scent of her hair.

Beneath his palm he felt the tightening of her nipple, lower down, his own natural response caused the muscles in her body to flex sensually. He allowed his thumb to replace his palm and began a slow circling of that pretty rosebud tip. Her pulse began to quicken, her breathing altered pace. On a muffled groan he nuzzled deeper into silken tresses until he found her nape.

Her response was to twist around until she was facing him. Their eyes met. He knew what his were saying, but hers were still trying to fight it.

'You don't play fair!' she protested.

'*Grazie,*' he replied, as if she had just paid him a great compliment, and claimed her mouth with a kiss aimed to kill any kind of argument.

What followed was an in-depth demonstration as to

why what they had was too special to throw away. It was hot and it was good, and as his body hardened with masculine arousal hers began to soften to a sensual pliancy that invited any intimacy.

She was beautiful. He adored her. No other woman had ever made him feel this deeply. He kissed every sweet sensational inch of her until she gave up trying to hate what he was doing and, on a helpless sigh, began to join in. What she found she couldn't reach with her mouth, she touched with tender knowing fingers. By the time he took final possession she was his entirely; there was no doubt about it. He watched her build towards her climax, he watched her reach and tumble into it, and he held her there. With gritted teeth and burning loins he held her, held her in magical suspension for as long as he could possibly manage it. Only when she eventually opened her eyes to look at him in dazed astonishment did he surrender and give her back what she had just given him.

Himself. He gave himself.

It really was the perfect moment to glide past everything that had gone before it and just be content to drift into sleep on the soft cloud of knowledge that neither of them was going to throw this away.

Lying there, with her cheek resting in the hollow of his shoulder and her hand covering the steady beat of his heart, escape into sleep was certainly all that Antonia wanted to do.

But Marco didn't agree. He was basking in self-confidence again, and that set his brain working. 'Tell me what Anton Gabrielli is to you,' he said, and very effectively shattered the peace.

'You just can't stop yourself, can you?' she snapped, pulling away from him to sit up with a sigh.

'I don't like mysteries,' he explained. 'And you knew the man, *cara*, no matter what you try to say.'

Knew him? A short laugh accompanied the weary shake of her head. Well, she mused bleakly, did she tell him and get it over with, or was this one secret better kept to herself? 'My mother was his mistress years ago.' She went for the compromise with part of the truth. 'He set her up in an apartment in Naples, visited her regularly, and took her out with his friends. He adored her on the face of it—but forgot to tell her he was married. When she found out, she left him.' That seemed the simplest way of saying it.

'You were around to witness this?' Quiet though it was, huskily gentle though it was, Antonia knew what he was thinking.

Learn by example.

'Yes, I was around,' she answered, while her fingers plucked at pale blue sheeting. Then, with a toss of her head, she made herself look at him. 'So you see, it was just another case of mistaken identity,' she explained bitterly.

'Then we will make it a priority tomorrow to correct the mistake.'

It was just so typically arrogant of him. 'Are you planning to put an ad in the newspaper, Marco, announcing to the world that your mistress is not the Mirror Woman? And do you honestly think anyone will believe you if you do?'

'We can at least try to set the record straight.'

'For what purpose?' she asked. 'To make *you* feel better? Your mother? *Me*? Don't you see? It doesn't matter who the model is; people will always look at me and see the same woman! I can't change that. I *look* like her! In every way but name I could *be* her! Either you have to learn to accept it or we have nothing left here to—'

Firm hands toppled her back down to him. 'Shut up,' he gritted. 'I know what you were going to say, so just shut up!'

'You started it,' she sighed.

'And I am finishing it!' And he did, by launching into a second seduction.

It was all very fierce, intense and possessive, but sex didn't solve everything. Okay, so in bed they were as compatible as any two human beings could be. But out of it?

Nothing could change. He wanted to fix what couldn't be fixed. Which was why she hadn't told him the full truth about Anton Gabrielli. She might love Marco, but some secrets you could only trust to someone who would love you enough not to care what you had to tell them.

And Marco didn't love her that way.

This time her drift from satiation to sleep was allowed to happen uninterrupted. But Marco lay awake, frowning into the darkness until dawn eventually began to filter into the room, when, carefully untangling himself from Antonia, he slid out of the bed.

Two hours later he was in a helicopter heading for his parents' Tuscany home, intent on an interview with his father. And Antonia was just awakening to find the place beside her empty—if you didn't count the written note waiting on the pillow.

'Don't worry me, *cara*,' it said. 'Be here when I return.'

Don't worry me, she read again. *Be here…*

Such emotive words, she thought sadly. But what did they tell her, except that he didn't want her to go? They didn't solve anything. They didn't put right what his mother had done to her self-esteem. She would have to be really brazen to go amongst his friends after last night's public humiliation and boldly outface their new perception of her.

And she wasn't that brazen. Though she didn't think Marco would understand if she tried to explain it to him. He would probably think she was angling after another marriage proposal. When in actual fact the one he'd given her had been more than enough for her.

So was she going to 'be here' when he got back?

Her indecisive sigh told its own story. She just couldn't make up her mind. To go was going to hurt. To stay was going to hurt. Her problem was deciding which one was going to hurt more.

Getting out of bed, she showered and dressed in a simple dusky-mauve skirt and a cerise top, then went to search out Carlotta to see if she knew where Marco had gone.

It was Saturday, after all, and she had rarely known him to work on Saturdays. He preferred to laze around and do as little as possible.

Carlotta was just placing a pot of coffee, a bowl of freshly sliced fruit and some toast down on the table for her when she arrived in the sunny breakfast room.

No, she didn't know where Marco had gone.

The smell of the toast made Antonia realise that with last night's drama she hadn't eaten a scrap since late afternoon yesterday and she was hungry, which was a much simpler problem to solve.

Or was it that she didn't really want to look for the answer to where Marco had gone? she wondered as she sat down. He'd threatened to go and see Anton Gabrielli. He also had to smooth things out with his mother. Who else? she asked herself. Confront Stefan with what she had told him? Demand his money back for the *Mirror Woman*? The list could go on and on.

Any interview between Marco and Anton Gabrielli did not sit comfortably with her, although the man could only tell Marco more or less what she had already said, she attempted to reassure herself.

As for an interview with his mother—the outcome of that depended entirely on which one of them was the more committed to his or her offended senses. Either way, it did not promise to be a pleasant conversation. Nor did it sit comfortably with her that she was the cause of dissension between mother and son.

Then there was Stefan. Annoyingly unpredictable Stefan, who was likely to say anything if Marco pushed hard enough. And, since he knew just about everything about her, it was yet another confrontation she would prefer didn't take place.

Which leaves you with what? she asked herself as she poured a second coffee. All of these people discussing you as if you didn't have a voice of your own? When all it would take is for you to face the man and tell him everything, warts and all, then stand back and see what the full truth brings you back by return.

Maybe she would. Maybe she would wait around after all, do just that, and tell Marco everything.

Carlotta appeared. 'A Signor Gabrielli is in the foyer, *signorina*,' she informed her. 'He is asking if you can spare him a few minutes of your time?'

Signor Gabrielli. Her stomach turned over. The coffee suddenly lost flavour. He couldn't know—could he? No, she told herself firmly. He couldn't know. He was here to ask about Anastasia, probably. Wanting to find out how his ex-mistress had faired in the twenty-five years since they'd last met!

Well, she was ready to tell him that, Antonia resolved, and came to her feet. 'Let him come up and show him into the small sitting room, Carlotta, if you please.'

The sheer formality of her words set the housekeeper frowning. The way Antonia's face had suddenly turned so cold caused a hesitation before Carlotta turned away without saying whatever had been on her mind.

Alone again, Antonia made herself sit down, made herself sip at the coffee and eat a piece of toast. And she made herself ready for a meeting that was coming twenty-five years too late.

CHAPTER NINE

HE WAS wearing a dark suit, white shirt and dark tie. And Antonia's first impression as she stepped into the room was—stiff. In the single grainy newspaper cutting she had of him he didn't look stiff. He looked young and vital—very much as Marco looked.

But that had been taken twenty years ago. In twenty years maybe cynicism with life could change Marco into this man's image. Though she hoped to goodness that it didn't, she thought with a distinct shiver.

'Good morning, *signor*,' she greeted him in cool English. 'I believe you wanted to see me?'

Gracious, polite, giving no hint that she knew anything at all about him. She was leaving it up to him to give away as much—or as little—as he knew about her.

He didn't return the greeting. In fact he didn't do anything but narrow his eyes and look her over like something in a specimen jar. Her nerve-ends began to tighten. He had a face cast from iron and a thin-lipped mouth that appeared to have forgotten how to smile. Already predisposed to dislike him, what she was feeling bouncing back from him gave her no reason to alter that view.

'You are Anastasia's daughter,' he eventually announced, as if he'd needed that detailed scrutiny to make absolutely sure before he committed himself to the statement.

'Yes,' she confirmed. 'Is it about my mother that you wish to see me?'

He shifted his stance. It wasn't by much but it was enough for her to know that he was intensely uncomfortable at being here. '*Si,*' he replied. 'And—no,' he added. 'By your response, I have to assume that you know about me?'

'Your affair with my mother? Yes.' She saw no reason to hide it.

He nodded in acknowledgement. 'It was perhaps unfortunate that we should meet as we did last night.'

Unfortunate? 'I think I shocked you,' she allowed. 'And I'm sorry for doing that.'

His eyes contained a distinctly cynical glint at her apology. 'Until I saw you I believed the Stefan Kranst paintings were your mother. But then,' he said curtly, 'I did not know that you existed.'

For the first time someone had made the correct assumption about Stefan's model. It was ironic that he was now changing his mind to suit what everyone else believed.

'We were extremely alike,' she said. 'Few people could tell the difference.'

'Were—?' he picked up sharply.

'My mother died two years ago,' she explained.

'I'm sorry for your loss,' he murmured politely.

'Thank you,' she replied. This couldn't become any more formal if they tried.

Shouldn't she be feeling something? Antonia asked herself curiously. Shouldn't she at least sense a genetic bond, even if it was only a small one? Realising she was still standing by the door, she began to walk forwards, gauging his tensing response as a man very much on his guard. What did he think she was going to do—physically attack him?

'You even walk like her,' he uttered.

Antonia just offered a brief smile. He wasn't telling her anything she didn't already know. She looked like her mother. She moved like her mother.

'Would you care to sit down?' she invited politely. 'Can I offer you a drink—espresso or—?'

'I am your father,' he ground out brusquely, bringing her to a breathtaking stop. Then, with a slash of a hand, 'There,' he said. 'It is now in the open between us. So we may stop this civility. What do you want?'

'I b-beg your pardon?' Antonia blinked in astonishment.

'You heard me,' he said. 'I want to know your price.'

Antonia could not believe she was hearing this. 'But you came to see me,' she reminded him. 'I didn't—'

'It is called pre-empting your intentions,' he cut in. 'I decided that it would only be a matter of time before you came after me. So here I am.' He gave a shrug. 'All I want to know is how much your silence is going to cost me.'

Her silence? Antonia stared at him in disbelief. He had come here to face her because he thought she was about to start blackmailing him? 'But I don't w-want—'

'Your kind always want.'

Suddenly it hurt to breathe. His voice held contempt. His eyes held contempt. He hated the sight of her! He didn't even know her yet he was judging her to be mercenary. And, *her kind*? A flashback came to her of Marco's mother wearing the same expression, showing the same arrogant superiority that they thought gave them the right to treat her like this!

Glancing up, he caught her expression; his own turned graven. 'Anastasia let me down,' he ground out bitterly. 'You should not be here. It is most unfortunate that we have to have this conversation at all.'

Was he saying what she thought he was saying? Sickness began to claw at her stomach. 'You thought my mother would go back to England and rid herself of me simply because it was what you expected her to do?'

'Anastasia demanded money,' he explained. 'I automatically assumed she meant to use it to—rectify the problem.'

The *problem*? 'I was not my mother's problem!' she cried. '*You* were that! She needed money to survive!' God, she felt so disgusted. 'You walked away, closed the lease on her apartment, bank accounts, *everything*!'

'It is the way these things work.' He was callously unrepentant. 'As you will find out yourself, no doubt, when your moment arrives.'

Was this how he had treated her mother on that final confrontation? Was this the reason why she never really recovered her self-esteem? How could she have loved this man? How could she have *not* seen through him?

'You make me feel sick,' she breathed.

'Don't take the high moral ground with me, *signorina*!' he suddenly barked at her. 'For here you are, living with a man who makes you the scornful talk of all Milan!' His face was hard again, his accent cold and his opinion of her set in stone. 'Think before you speak, whether you would prefer *me* to announce to the world that Marco Bellini's mistress is Anton Gabrielli's bastard daughter! And the Mirror Woman is actually her cheap slut of a mother!'

She slapped him—hard. For which part she wasn't sure, but the hand flew out when he insulted her mother. Standing there facing each other, both emanated intense dislike, and she did not feel even a small hint of remorse for that slap. His hand came up to cover his cheek and his eyes burned vows of revenge on her.

'I heard what Isabella Bellini did to you last night,' he said. 'The whole gallery was buzzing with talk of the incident.' And he smiled that thin smile again when she turned white. 'Do you think you will still be here if this situation ever becomes public?' he posed. 'Do you think because you can lay claim to a father worth as much as the Bellinis they will turn a blind eye to what you actually are?'

'How can you stand there and preach over me when your own sins are staring right at you?' Antonia gasped. 'And why come here at all, if you don't care if I speak out? You have a wife. Don't her feelings count for anything?'

'My wife is dead,' he said. 'You cannot hurt her. But I can most certainly hurt your present position here in this place of luxury if you dare to make our connection public.'

'But I don't understand why you should think I'd want to!' The whole thing had become so bewildering, she couldn't follow his logic at all.

'I don't,' he said. 'I merely wanted to be sure that you understand your position here. For you don't have one.' He made the point plain. 'I am no use to you as a lever towards marriage to Bellini. In fact I am most probably your biggest danger to that goal. But I am willing to accept you possess a certain right to lay embarrassment at my doorstep,' he conceded. 'And, bearing in mind that one day in the future Bellini is going to tire of you, I accept I owe you some—incentive to keep your silence about me when that time comes.'

'I want you to leave,' she announced, beginning to shake on the inside.

'This is not your home to order me out of,' he replied, and at last his thin lips did what she suspected they had been wanting to do since he arrived here and twisted into bitter dislike. 'Just name your own figure…'

Staring at him, she realised he'd had the absolute gall to reach into his inside pocket and take out his cheque-book! He was expecting to pay her off! Anger returned, and she was glad to feel it rise up inside her because it saved her from bursting into tears.

He was standing there with book and pen, waiting for her to say something. So she did. It was really too irresistible not to. 'Everything you're worth,' she announced, then folded her arms and watched his face turn to plastic. Money, it seemed, was all-important to him. Oh—and his reputation, she added, since he really couldn't cope with the idea of having a twenty-five-year-old mistake come back to haunt him!

Irritation flashed across his face. 'I don't think you understand—'

'My own worth?' she put in. 'Or how much *you* are worth *signor*?' She took delight in watching him stiffen. 'Well, let me put that question straight before there is any more confusion here. You are worth precisely *nothing* to me—*capisce*?' She even used Marco's way of saying it. 'So you may write on your cheque "I give my illegitimate daughter Antonia Carson exactly *nothing*!"' Her eyes flashed with disgust. 'Now excuse me,' she said, and turned and left the room.

If Marco had been there to watch her do it, he would have recognised the move as Antonia showing her contempt.

But Marco wasn't here. And neither did she intend to be by the time he arrived home. If her own father could view her like that, what hope did she ever have of gaining the respect of anyone while she continued to stay with Marco?

She had to go—and right now, she decided. Before Marco had any chance of convincing her otherwise! And the saddest thing was she knew he could do it. One word, one touch, and she was as weak as a kitten where it involved him.

Carlotta was hovering in the hallway. Her face looked concerned, which made Antonia wonder if the housekeeper had overheard what had been said in the sitting room.

But, 'Will you see Signor Gabrielli out for me, please?' was all Antonia said to her. Then walked past her and into the bedroom...

At about the same time that she was confronting her father, Marco was confronting his own across the desk in the family library. All around them stood the results of centuries of time-honoured collecting. The house itself was a national treasure. And out beyond the window spread a whole valley strung with the vines which made the wine the Bellini name was as famous for as its centuries-old corporate leadership.

'I need your support,' Marco was saying grimly. 'I have no wish to feud with my own parents, but push me and I will.' It was both a threat and a warning.

'You are expecting me to dictate to your mother?' the older man asked, then released a laugh of fond derision. 'Sorry, Marco. But I am too sick and too wise to accept the task.'

But he wasn't as sick as Marco had expected to find him. 'You're looking better,' he remarked—perhaps belatedly.

'Thank you for noticing.' His father thought it belated

too. In height, in looks, in every way there could be, Marco was his father's son. But a few months ago a virus had sucked the life out of Federico Bellini. By the time the doctors had managed to stabilise him he had halved his body weight, lost the use of one lung and damaged his heart, liver and kidneys.

'New drugs,' the older man dismissed with the same contempt with which he had always treated the medication which kept him living. 'Who is this woman your mother sees as such a threat that she publicly offends her?'

Subject of his health over, Marco noted. It was his father's way. It would be Marco's way, given the same circumstances. 'You know who she is,' he sighed. 'She's been living with me for the last year.'

'You mean you're still with the same one?' Federico pretended to be shocked, but Marco wasn't taken in by it. Though he did allow himself a wry little smile of appreciation for the thrust. 'No wonder your mother is in a panic.'

'It isn't her place to panic.'

'Then I repeat,' his father incised, 'who is she?' And the accent was most definitely on the *who*.

Dipping his hand into his inside pocket, it was not a chequebook that Marco retrieved, but a photograph, taken at his best friend's wedding. He dropped it on the desk in front of his father. Federico picked it up, studied it.

'Your good taste has never been in question,' he drawled.

'But—?' Marco prompted.

'I might have been out of circulation for the last year, but I have seen the painting,' Federico said. 'She has an exquisite body and sad eyes.' The photograph came back across the desk.

Odd, Marco noted, that when he could have challenged that comment with the truth he did nothing of the kind.

Because Antonia was right, he realised. Look at the naked mother and you see the naked daughter. So it didn't really matter what people were told.

And anyway, there was a point of honour here he was determined to hold on to. He had a right to choose his own future, and Antonia had a right to be accepted for that choice. If his parents could not bring themselves to do that, then...

Then what? he asked himself.

'Nice to own. Nice to sip,' his father murmured. 'But that's about all, Marco...'

It was a refusal of support. Marco picked up the photograph and placed it back in his pocket. 'Is that your final word?'

His father sent him a grim look as he stood up to leave. 'Is she pregnant?' he asked.

Now there was an interesting concept, Marco mused cynically. A Bellini child, born out of wedlock. A wry smile touched his mouth 'No,' he replied. 'But I could easily make it so.'

Ah—now he was actually being taken seriously, he saw with grim satisfaction as his father's expression sharpened dramatically. 'Sit down,' Federico commanded.

Marco complied, but only because it was what he had expected to be told when he'd stood up in the first place.

'Now, explain to me why *this* woman, when you could have any woman you wanted?'

Arrogance abounded. Antonia would have just loved

to hear his father say those words. 'She's what I want.' He stated it simply. Then he sat forward and looked his father directly in the eye. 'She is what I intend to have,' he extended with deadly seriousness. *'Comprende…?'*

The silence lasted for all of thirty seconds, the sabre fight with their eyes an evenly matched thing. Then Federico Bellini sat back in his thick brown leather chair, huffed out a short laugh, gave a shake of his head and said, 'Next weekend. Here, I think. We will keep this official, above-board and on the right side of the sheets, if you don't mind.'

'Grazie,' Marco thanked him, and not by a flicker did he wallow in his triumph.

But his father hadn't finished. His eyes suddenly took on a devilish gleam. 'Now all you have to do is get your mother to see things your way…'

Carlotta had already been in and returned the bedroom to its usual pristine smoothness, Antonia found. Nothing out of place, nothing to show that the room had been used at all. Walking over to a built-in closet, she took out the small leather suitcase again. She wasn't really surprised to find that Marco had neatly returned her clothes to their appropriate places in the room. It was the way of the man. The way of his housekeeper. Everything neat and in its place. This bedroom was Antonia's place. Last night should have reminded her of that.

This time no angry male strode in to halt the process of packing. The suitcase closed with a snap. But as she set the case down on the floor a knock sounded on the door and Carlotta stepped inside.

Of course, she had to see the suitcase. Her eyes shot to Antonia's. 'No, *signorina*, you—'

Something stopped her. An awareness of her place in the order of things? Acceptance that, for Antonia at any rate, leaving was perhaps the wise thing for her to do?

Looking away again, she walked forward. 'Signor Gabrielli asked me to give you this,' she said, and handed Antonia a cheque, then turned and left again without uttering another word.

It kind of said it all. Without so much as glancing at the cheque to see how much money her father considered his daughter's silence worth, she ripped it into small pieces and deposited it in the waste-paper basket, then, simply because she needed to do it, she walked over to the terrace window and stepped outside.

Milan shimmered in the blistering heat of yet another hot summer's day. Way down there below her the traffic made up for its unusual silence of the night before. And one of the first things her eyes fell upon was the imprint of Marco's body still hugging the cushions on the lounger he must have used. Carlotta had obviously not got around to coming out here yet, because a sandwich and a glass of red wine were standing on a table close by.

When he hadn't been able to sleep last night, he must have gone to the kitchen to make himself a late night snack and brought it out here to enjoy. But he'd seen her lying asleep on the other lounger. Food and wine had been forgotten in favour of other forces.

Like the recovery of his woman, she mused. The putting her back where she belonged, in his arms, and in his bed.

Her eyes glazed over. She had to turn away to stop the tears from flowing. It was then that she remembered the tear-drop diamond necklace, and set her feet moving further down the terrace to find it still lying exactly where she had placed it beneath the lounger. Recovering it, she took it back into the bedroom and was about to put it down on her dressing table when she noticed the note from Marco folded there.

'Don't worry me, *cara*,' it said. 'Be here when I return.'

It came without warning. The first sob, followed quickly by another—and another. Dropping onto the dressing stool, she covered her face with her hands then simply let go and sobbed her heart out.

When it was over, she stood up. Took a moment to compose herself and decide what she needed to do before she left here for the last time...

Marco was standing alone in his father's library, using the landline telephone to connect him with the Romano Gallery. He wanted Stefan Kranst. He got Rosetta Romano.

'Where is he?' he demanded.

'He flies home to England this afternoon,' Rosetta told him. 'I thought you must know that he never meant to stay longer than the first-night viewing. What do you want me to do with Signorina Carson's painting?' she asked. 'Stefan never said, and Signorina Carson rang off before I could ask her when she called looking for Stefan not ten minutes ago.'

The painting. Marco frowned. He'd forgotten all about it. 'Have it packed up and delivered to my apartment,' he instructed. 'Did Antonia say why she wanted Kranst?'

'No. She just asked where he was staying and rang off, that was all.'

Marco rang off too. It wasn't that he was worried any longer about Stefan Kranst, he told himself. But his feet took him in search of his father to wish him a quick farewell before he was heading outside and to the waiting helicopter. It didn't occur to him, until he was in the air again, that he could have rung Antonia before leaving, just to check that she was okay.

Okay, he then repeated drily. You want to check that she's actually there! He didn't trust her. Could he trust her? 'This changes nothing,' she had told him in the depths of a night of loving. Impulsively he fished out his mobile. One glance from his pilot and he was reluctantly putting it away again.

Antonia was arguing with Stefan. 'You have to do this for me, Stefan—please,' she begged him. 'You *owe* it to me after last night's fiasco!'

'Isabella Bellini was contrite afterwards, if that helps you any,' he told her.

'I don't care what she was!' It was almost a sob. 'It doesn't make any difference. My mind is made up. I'm leaving Milan.'

'And Marco?' he included.

She swallowed and nodded. 'These are the keys.' Her fingers shook as she held them out to him. 'All you need to do is pay off the lease then get my things and bring them with you back to London.'

Stefan refused to take the keys. 'What in heaven's name happened after you left with him?' he demanded impatiently.

But she shook her head. 'I'll tell you another time. I have a plane to catch.'

'Does he know you're going?' Stefan asked.

She didn't answer. He released a sigh. 'My darling, I've told you something like this before but I am going to say it again. Marco Bellini is not a man to cross swords with.'

Her chin shot up, jewel-bright eyes sparkling with something he had never seen there before. It was bitter, blinding, gut-wrenching cynicism. 'Is that your way of saying that *you* don't want to cross swords with him?'

'My God,' Stefan breathed, and took the keys. 'Go,' he said. 'Go!' he repeated. 'I'll follow on tomorrow if I can get a flight. But go if you must.'

'Thank you,' she whispered, kissed his cheek and left his hotel suite without looking back again. If she had done she would have hesitated, because Stefan was wearing a look fit to slay any dragon that might be threatening her.

And she didn't want Marco slayed. She needed to know he was alive and happy. In fact, it was essential to her own sanity that he remained exactly the way she wanted to remember him. Tall and lean and suave and sophisticated, but wearing one of those lazy grins that oozed sex appeal. She wanted to remember him laughing with his friends. Talking seriously about art. Or lying on a sun lounger in the middle of the night with a glass of red wine and a sandwich—missing her.

Oh, yes, she needed him to miss her, she admitted, as her taxi began a battle with Milan's mad Saturday traffic.

She had managed to reserve a seat on a flight out of Linate airport, which was only four miles outside Milan. But it was tourist season and the roads to the airport were as busy as she had ever seen them. As the taxi eventually made it to the perimeter of the airport compound she glanced outside in time to catch the sun sparkling on a helicopter as it hovered just before landing.

Marco's preferred form of transport to his parents'

home, she recalled, with a sad little smile, and turned
away quickly, not wanting to think about Marco right
now when she could still weaken and change her mind.

Marco saw the traffic as he came in to land, and cursed
it. It was going to take an age to get back into the city
through all of that. With a quick thanks to his pilot he
got out of the helicopter and strode off towards the airport building. Any other time he would be heading for
the executive car park and jumping into his car. But the
Ferrari had been booked in for a service this morning,
so he'd had to come here by taxi. Which meant he now
had to walk right across the airport concourse to find
the nearest taxi rank.

If he'd thought about it, he could have used the Lotus
and saved himself a lot of hassle, because he had things
to do, people to see, before he could get back to
Antonia.

Which reminded him. Taking out his mobile, he tried
getting a signal. It was only when nothing happened that
he realised he'd forgotten to put the battery on charge
the night before. The damn thing was dead. Sighing, he
pocketed the phone again.

It was beginning to turn into one of those days.

The airport lounges were busy, packed to bursting
with newly arriving tourists. Taking the direct route towards the exit doors, he had to squeeze between people
and their luggage. There was a moment when he paused
though, half considering going to check in the other
lounge to see if Stefan Kranst was there. But he decided
he didn't have the time and kept on going towards the
exit.

Outside again, the queue for taxis was long.
Frustration bit into his patience while he waited with

the rest of them. As one cab drove off another took its place. The constant circling of people to and from Milan must be a very good earner, the banker in him decided.

At last he got his turn. Diving into the back of the cab, he gave his destination, then closed the door. As he sat back, he experienced the strangest sensation when he picked up the scent of Antonia's perfume.

On his clothes, on his skin? he wondered. Or was it so impregnated into his senses that it was always there? He liked that idea. It made him smile and relax while he let the driver take on the battle to get him where he needed to go.

To Buccellati's first, to find something that bit special for Antonia to wear on her finger. Then the less palatable task of taking on his mother…

By the time Antonia discovered that her flight had been delayed she was beginning to have second thoughts about running away like this. She didn't want to go. She didn't want to stay. She didn't know what she wanted to do!

Yes, you do, she told herself. You want to have everything go back to how it was. But it can't. Too much has happened.

I love him, though!

She lowered her head, glad she'd left her hair down because it helped to hide the tears swimming in her eyes. Her bag lay across her lap. She opened it up to hunt for a paper tissue. But what she came up with was a photograph taken at Nicola and Franco's wedding. She was standing next to Marco and he had his arm around her. She looked so happy. So did he, though not in the same way. Her happiness shone through with love, his shone with—

Sexual contentment.

She was right to go, she told herself.

But her mouth began to quiver, and the tears were beginning to spread.

Stefan thought she was making a mistake. He had been angry—disappointed with her, even. 'He'll strike back hard,' he'd warned her before at the de Maggio's anniversary party.

Oh, yes, please let him do that, she prayed, like the weak little fool that she was. Let him come for me, lock me up and throw away the key—I don't care! I *like* being his mistress! It's everyone else the job seems to offend!

Think of your mother, she grimly told herself. Think of Anton Gabrielli and how you could actually *see* Marco becoming like him in years to come! Then, no, she denied. That isn't true. If I was pregnant Marco wouldn't—

How do you *know* he wouldn't?

She didn't know, and that was the ugly little truth which kept her pinned to the chair in the airport lounge instead of getting up and running back to him. Anton Gabrielli had planted a lot of ugliness into her heart, she realised. The contempt, the accusations, the automatic belief that she must be out for all she could get. He'd despised her mother just for *being*! He despised her in the same way. So did Marco's mother.

Her chin jerked up. It was a strange sensation, but her heart suddenly felt as if someone had walked past and wiped it clean as a slate!

Only a mother could do that. Only a mother had the power to wipe another woman clean of any aspirations towards her son. So maybe it was because of Isabella Bellini's contempt that she was still sitting on this chair.

For, without her blessing, any relationship with Marco would be sordid from now on.

It hadn't felt sordid last night. It had been beautiful last night. It had been special. Marco had made it special. 'Don't worry me,' he'd written. 'Be here when I return.'

Her heart gave a squeeze. As the muscles relaxed again, all the warmth and feelings of love came flooding back in. Glancing down, she saw the photograph still clutched in her hands. The tears came back. The indecision. She wished they would call her flight. She needed to go—get away from here!

Marco strode into the apartment building and headed directly for the lift. He'd had a good day in a lot of ways. A real *coup d'état*! But it had taken too much time, and now he was anxious to see Antonia, begin to put things on a proper footing for them at last.

As the lift took him up with its usual smoothness he found himself smiling when his hand coiled round the small ring box in his pocket. The lift stopped, the doors slid open. He strode out. This was it, he told himself as he opened the apartment door. The most important few minutes of his life were about to happen!

Strangely, he'd never expected it to feel this good.

Stepping inside, the first thing he saw was the large brown cord-wrapped package leaning against the wall—Antonia's portrait he'd had delivered from the Romano Gallery. The next thing was Carlotta. She was standing there wringing her hands. Ice cold struck right through to his heart.

'Antonia?' he rasped. 'Where is she?'

The housekeeper's eyes were filled with dismay. 'She's gone, *signor*,' she whispered. 'She's gone...'

CHAPTER TEN

His legs took him down the hall, into the bedroom and straight to the built-in cupboard. The suitcase had gone. Through the eyes of a man who was still not prepared to take in what was happening to him, he turned to scan the rest of the room.

What had once pleased his eye, with its uninterrupted use of space, now looked cold and spartan, as if someone had come along and wiped it clean of its heartbeat.

So the few small items carefully placed on the smooth bed caught his attention. Walking over to them, he just stood staring down at the set of keys to this apartment, the tear-drop diamond necklace, the stack of credit cards and the mobile telephone.

His skin suddenly felt as if it didn't fit his body any more. Was that all she felt she was worth to him? Even the bed was playing its part here. He began to feel sick. If she'd tossed down a set of scarlet underwear she could not have made her feelings more clear.

The phone gave a beep. He looked at it, saw there was a message written on it in text. Picking it up he stared at the words she had left for him. 'I'm sorry,' was all that it said.

In English too. He sometimes forgot she spoke English her Italian was so good. But, maybe in this case *I'm sorry* said it better for her than *mi despiace* did.

It didn't for him, because *sorry* wasn't enough! He wanted to know more. He wanted to know *why*! Could she not have held faith with him for just one more day?

'When did she leave?' He was aware of Carlotta standing in the doorway, watching him with anxious eyes. She obviously had something to tell him or she wouldn't be there invading his private moment like this.

'Just after the *signor* left,' the housekeeper answered.

Signor. Marcos swung round. 'Signor Kranst?' he demanded.

But Carlotta shook her head. 'A Signor Gabrielli,' she informed him. 'I think they argued,' she added, looking uncomfortable for saying so. 'The *signorina* had me see him out. It is when he gave me the cheque to give to Signorina Antonia.' Her eyes flickered, then dropped to the waste-paper basket standing by the dressing table. 'She was very upset,' she added, as Marco's gaze followed hers to the basket.

A bell sounded then, saying that someone was in the foyer wanting to come up. 'I don't want to see anyone,' Marco grimly instructed.

With a nod, Carlotta left, leaving him alone to walk over to the waste-paper basket.

About the same time that Stefan was using tough talk on Carlotta to gain his way into the apartment, Antonia's flight was being called at last.

It was now two hours late and her nerves were completely frazzled. Gathering her things together, she stood up, then paused to take in a careful breath. This was it, she told herself. She could leave now. No more arguing with herself. No more agonising over what she really wanted to do. It had to be better to go while she still had the strength to do it, rather than wait until she was thrown out then spend five years pining for his return, as her mother had—wasn't it?

So move, Antonia, she told her feet. Follow the general exodus towards the gate as if you're just another tourist on her way back home.

'No luggage slip, *signorina*?'

She looked down at the cabin-weight suitcase which suddenly seemed a pathetic judgement on her year in Milan. When she'd packed it, in London, she had meant to send for her other things once she was settled with Marco. But he had done away with the need by buying her new things. Anything else of value to her would be coming back to London with Stefan.

She shook her head at the attendant who was checking her boarding pass. 'This is all I have,' she said. And a heart full of tears, she added silently.

Marco was leaning against the open window, which led out onto the terrace, when Stefan Kranst had the arrogance to stride into the room.

'I want words with you,' he insisted grimly. 'I don't know what happened last night after you left Romano's with Antonia. But—'

'Anton Gabrielli happened,' Marco inserted, without bothering to turn.

The name met with silence. Not the blank, who-are-you-talking-about kind of silence. But the dear-God-in-heaven kind, that throbbed with grim recognition.

'What did he want?' Stefan asked him.

'I see you know the man,' Marco drily responded.

'What did he want?' Stefan repeated harshly.

His anger jolted Marco enough for him to wave a hand towards the bed. 'See for yourself,' he invited. And turned to study Stefan Kranst's face as he walked over to look down at the neat row of items set out on the bed. The diamond, the keys, the credit cards, the phone still displaying its message. And the cheque, carefully pieced back together. Stefan stared at it for a long time before he spoke.

'I saw him at the gallery last night,' he admitted. 'I hoped you'd got Antonia away before he arrived.'

'They came face to face. He called her Anastasia...'

Other than for a tightening of his lips, Stefan made no comment. 'When did this arrive?' he asked grimly instead.

'The man delivered it himself this morning,' Marco told him, 'while I was out,'

'No wonder she left in a hurry. He threatened her, didn't he?' Hard eyes lifted to Marco. 'Do you know who he is?'

The question earned him a grimace. 'Her father, at a guess.'

'She told you that?' Stefan looked so surprised that Marco couldn't hold back the wry smile.

'No,' he admitted. 'I managed to work it out.' She didn't feel able to trust me with it, he added silently, and sent his gaze flicking back to the view beyond the terrace. She hadn't really trusted him with anything, when he came to think about it. Not the truth about the *Mirror Woman*. Not the father he hadn't known she had. Even her innocent relationship with Kranst had been kept a titillating secret.

Out there, above the city, he saw a flash of light as the sun caught the tips of a plane as it took off. 'Do you know where she is?' he asked quietly.

'Not on that flight, if that's what you're thinking,' Stefan Kranst replied. 'She left for England hours ago, Marco,' he added almost gently.

The gentleness was almost his undoing. Moisture dared to slide across his eyes. He stiffened up, shoved his hands in his pockets, heaved in a deep breath. Felt the ring box, felt some other emotion wreak havoc with the wall of his chest.

'I'm going after her,' he announced, keeping his face turned away from Kranst as he shifted towards the bed-room door.

'I came here for a reason,' Stefan reminded him.

Marco paused. 'To gloat?' he suggested.

Stefan released a heavy sigh. 'Give me a break for once, Marco,' he begged wearily. 'I *care* about Antonia more than her real father does. That means I *care* about what's been happening here! She came to see me before she left,' he went on tightly. 'I didn't like the way she looked. Now I know why, if Gabrielli's been here,' he added cynically. 'But the point is, she gave me some-thing I think you should know about...'

Marco spun around.

'Keys.' Stefan took them out of his pocket. 'And an address in Milan. I came to see if you were as interested as I am in finding out what the hell she has been keep-ing from *both* of us!'

She couldn't do it.

Standing here at the departure gate, with her boarding pass in her hand and only a short walk to freedom, she couldn't take another single step!

Tears clogged her throat, burned her eyes, hurt her stomach. I love him! she cried inside, and just couldn't go!

'Are you all right?' someone asked her. Someone else pushed impatiently past. 'You don't look well, *signo-rina*...'

I'm not. I'm sick with love. 'I've just r-remembered s-something,' she murmured shakily. 'I have to go back to Milan.' She swallowed at the attendant's shocked expression. 'Can you take my name off the f-flight register, please? I have my luggage here with me so you d-don't have to have it removed from the plane.'

Maybe that was why she'd used the smallest suitcase she could find. Maybe she *never* intended leaving Marco! Maybe she'd needed to get this far before she could finally accept that the man was her other half! You couldn't go anywhere with only half of you! It just wouldn't let you.

Dropping the tickets and the boarding pass on the attendant's desk, she turned and started running. She needed to get back to him—fast! 'Don't worry me,' he'd said. 'Be here when I return!'

He wanted her. What more could she ask of him, for goodness' sake? He *cared* that his mother had upset her! He had even asked her to marry him so that she wouldn't leave!

Oh God, why did clarity have to come this late? Why couldn't she have just waited until he got home and then faced him with Anton Gabrielli, instead of running away without giving him a chance to respond? And he *wasn't* like Gabrielli! How dared she compare the two of them?

The taxi queue was huge. Strange therefore, after a half-hour wait, she should get the same driver that had brought her to the airport. She gave the address for the apartment. He raised his eyebrows at her via the mirror as he drove off. 'It is a popular address today, *signorina.* I collected you from there this morning,' he remembered. 'Then I took another person there this afternoon. Now I take you back. Do you think the gentleman will be waiting to catch my taxi for the return journey here?'

He thought it was funny. Antonia didn't. 'Do you know the man's name?' she questioned huskily.

'Sure,' he shrugged. 'Everyone knows Signor Bellini. He tips well too...'

Marco paid off the driver and got out of the taxi to wait for Stefan to join him. The Ferrari wasn't back from its service and he was damned if he was going to drive Antonia's Lotus. That was staying exactly where it was until *she* came back to claim it.

'What the hell has she been doing in a place like this?' he demanded.

Stefan didn't answer. Going to the door, he used the key, then stepped inside. With Marco crowding behind him he took the stairs floor by floor, passing by the doors bearing nameplates of a suspect nature.

'You do know that this is part of the red-light district?' Marco growled into Stefan's back.

'I do now,' the other man answered and, though he had a fair idea what it was that Antonia did here, he was beginning to feel a trifle edgy—just in case he was wrong.

They arrived on the top landing. Neither spoke as they stepped up to the only door. Stefan turned the key, the tension riding high as he walked inside first.

Therefore he had those few split seconds to just stand looking around him before murmuring, 'Well, that's a relief.' Then he added a rueful grin.

Not for Marco it wasn't. How long had he known this woman? he asked himself as he stood there beside Stefan Kranst and stared at what might euphemistically be called an artist's studio. Light streamed in through a wall of windows, setting dust motes dancing in the air. The room smelled of old wood and oil and turpentine thinner, and everywhere you looked stood the paintings. Some drying, some framed, some waiting to be framed. Piazza del Duomo. La Scala. Pusteria di Sant'Ambrogio. The bustling Brera, with its trendy little shops and people, and the gardens at Villa Reale.

Over by the window stood a huge trestle bench stacked with pencil sketches. On the easel waited a half-finished view from his own terrace, looking out over the top of Milan.

Marco hadn't known Antonia had ever picked up a paintbrush, never mind possessed the capacity to produce work like this.

'Look at these,' Stefan murmured. He had moved towards the window and was now sifting through the sketches.

Sketches of life drawn with a quick sure hand. Sketches of people going about their business. Something caught in Marco's chest as he had a sudden vision of her sitting on a bench or a low stone wall just sketching—sketching while he had been safely out of the way in his office playing in the big league, believing her to be doing what the women of wealthy men did, which was basically nothing.

Then—no. He amended that notion, and didn't like himself for admitting that he hadn't really given much thought to what Antonia did when he wasn't there.

Stefan lifted a sheet of paper to one side, then went still enough to catch Marco's attention. Marco's own face looked back at him. It almost took his breath away, at the accuracy with which she had caught his mood of the moment.

The shark on his way to hunt prey, he named it with a wryness that didn't hold any humour. Picking it up, he found another—and another. All revealing his different moods in accurate detail.

Then something else caught his eye to divert his at-

tention. It was a half-finished painting of Franco and
Nicola about to leave on their honeymoon. Antonia
clearly had not been pleased with the result because she
had tossed it onto the bench and left it there. But that
wasn't why the painting held him. It was the realisation
that, in size, it would have fitted exactly the painting
she had wrapped for the anniversary gift.

Yet she hadn't thought to show him, ask his approval.
In fact she hadn't sought his approval on anything she
had been doing in here.

And it hurt. 'Why not tell me?' he murmured out
loud.

Turning from where he had wandered off to, Stefan
Kranst looked at him—just looked—and he knew the
answer. She would have had to feel safe from his mockery to tell him about all of this, and she hadn't.

'I am no ogre,' he growled out angrily—angrily because this was just another area she hadn't trusted him
with.

Antonia had changed her mind at the very last minute.
She didn't know why she had done it, but some instinct
had suddenly spoken to her and said, Better stop Stefan
from emptying your studio if you're intending to stay
here. So she'd redirected the driver and realised only
after she had let him go that she no longer had any keys
to get into the building.

Fortunately another tenant was just coming out. He
recognised her and, with a smile, stood back to allow
her inside. 'You have visitors,' he told her.

Stefan. She smiled. *'Grazie,'* she said, and let him
close the door behind her.

Her case wasn't heavy, but she was puffing a bit by
the time she reached the top landing. The door was open

a little. Pushing it wider, she paused to put down her suitcase just as Marco growled out harshly, 'What did she think I was going to do—laugh in her face?'

Her breathing changed from an out-of-breath pant to a trembling stammer, her mouth ran dry, her eyes glazed. Marco was here, with Stefan, of all people. It felt as if fate was still controlling her actions like a puppet on a string.

'Well,' she managed to whisper, 'are you?'

He spun round to face the doorway. Silence roared, tension sung, the sunlight shone on his black silk hair. He was wearing slate-grey. Slate-grey suit, slate-grey shirt, darker slate-grey tie. His skin had a polished gold cast to it, and his eyes were the same colour as his tie— dark with anger and passion and hurt pride.

She wanted to break down and weep at the sheer beautiful sight of him. She wanted to go to him, wrap her arms around his neck and cling so tightly that he would never *ever* be able to shake her free.

But instead her chin went up, it simply had to. No matter how desperate she was to feel his touch, or how shaky she was feeling inside, or even how afraid she was of hearing his answer to the question—she had to challenge him with it. It was a matter of her own pride.

'You're on a plane,' he said. It was really stupid. It was the very last thing she'd expected him to say.

'I couldn't go.'

'I'm not laughing.' He answered her question.

'What I do here is important to me,' she told him.

'I can see that,' he answered. 'Why couldn't you go?'

Her eyelashes flickered. Everything felt as if it was coming to her through a confused mist. She wet her lips with her tongue, linked her fingers together in a trembling pleat across her trembling stomach.

'Y-you didn't want me to,' she murmured unsteadily. 'Y-you trusted me to stay but I didn't trust you to…' The words trailed away on a wash of distraction. 'Th-that s-sketch you're holding isn't a good likeness.' Her fingers unpleated so she could point to what he was holding in his hand.

He looked down at it like someone who had no idea that he was holding anything. 'You think I'm a shark,' he murmured as he looked back at her.

'Sometimes.' She nodded.

'Are you coming in, or are you thinking of running again?'

'Oh.' It was her turn to glance down as if she didn't know where she was or what she was doing. She was still standing on the threshold, with her case sitting beside her and her bag swinging from one of her shoulders.

She went to pick up the case. The moment she moved, so did Marco. He came across the bare-board floor at the speed of lightning. The case was lifted out of her reach. Her arm was imprisoned in long fingers. Before she knew what he was about she was fully inside the room and the door was being firmly closed behind her.

That was when she saw Stefan, leaning against a wall with his arms casually folded and his expression—interested. 'Hi,' she murmured self-consciously.

'Hi, yourself,' Stefan softly replied. 'I don't suppose you would like to explain what's been going on here?' he drily requested.

'She doesn't need to explain anything,' Marco put in tensely, and his hand tightened on her arm as if he expected her to break free and run, when in actual fact she was already hanging on to his shirt at his waistband and had no intention of letting go of it.

Stefan sent the dry look Marco's way. 'She does if you want me to get out of here,' he replied, without bothering to hide his meaning.

Marco grimaced and remained silent, conceding Stefan's right to demand an explanation.

Still shaking too much, and not thinking straight, it needed a few attempts at breathing properly before Antonia could find some semblance of intelligence.

'Y-you know I paint. You taught me to do it,' she reminded Stefan.

'You taught yourself,' he drily corrected. 'By being a pain in the neck and insisting on placing your easel next to mine every time I worked so you could copy my every damn brushstroke.'

'I *learned* from you then.' She sighed at the play with semantics.

'Not this kind of stuff,' he said with derision. 'This is chocolate-box art they sell on street corners.'

'It's art,' Marco sliced back at him in her defence.

It was sweet of him, but Stefan was right. 'Shops,' she corrected. 'I sell them to the shops on the Brera. They sell them to the tourists. It—it makes me a nice little living...'

'So that's why you hardly ever touched the money I gave you,' Marco said bleakly.

'And your serious work?' Stefan asked, refusing to be sidetracked.

She tensed up; so did Marco. 'What serious work?' he demanded.

'You saw an example of it last night,' Stefan informed him, without taking his eyes off Antonia's suddenly angry face.

'*Dio mio,*' Marco breathed, his eyes wide with surprise as he stared at her. 'You mean *you* painted your own nude study?'

'Sometimes I hate you,' she hissed at Stefan.

Stefan just shrugged, moved out of his lazy stance against the wall and began walking towards them. 'Ask her about the one she has stashed against the wall over there,' he suggested to Marco as he passed by them. Then he paused, leaned over to kiss Antonia's angry cheek. 'Pack the chocolate-box stuff in before you ruin yourself with it,' he warned seriously, then pulled open the door and left them to it.

Or left Antonia to stand there on her own while she watched Marco stride across the room to the large canvas Stefan had so kindly pointed out to him.

Her cheeks began to heat, her body to stiffen in readiness for what was to come. She tried to divert him. 'Marco, we need to talk…'

But it was already too late. 'Now, just look at what we have here,' he drawled lazily. And with a deft flick of his hands he scooped the painting up and took it over to her easel.

She struggled not to gasp. Her cheeks were on fire. Standing back, he proceeded to study the nude painting of himself with the all-seeing eye of the complete connoisseur.

When he started to grin, she felt like following Stefan. But the way he reached out and touched the lean shape of a sleek male thigh was pure infuriating conceit.

'It's all wrong,' she snapped. 'The proportions are out. Your nose looks like Caesar's and your torso is too long!'

'I think it's perfect.'

He would, she thought with an angry frown. 'I *hate* people looking at my work until it's finished!'

'You mean you hate *me* looking at it!' His mood changed so swiftly she wasn't prepared for it. From lazy conceit he was suddenly pulsing with fury. '*Why*?' he demanded, walking back to her. 'Why couldn't you tell me that you can paint like this? I thought I knew you! But I've been living with a stranger! Your mother sits on my wall but you don't bother to tell me that! Your ex-lover has never been your ex-lover! In fact, I bet you never even had a lover before me—did you?' She blushed and shook her head, which only infuriated him more. He continued heatedly, 'You have a rat for a father. And you have a gift at your fingertips that I would have thought you would have been *proud* to let me see!'

'You own a Rembrandt!' she fired at him defensively.

'I own a Kranst!' he threw right back. 'Many works by totally unknown artists. *And* the Rembrandt! Are you saying I am an art snob on top of all my other failings?'

'Your opinion meant too much to me!' she cried. 'So it was safer not to seek it!'

He grabbed her and kissed her. And about time too, she thought as she fell into the kiss like a woman starved.

'*Dio mio,*' he rasped against her clinging lips. 'Do you have any idea what it did to me to come back and find you gone today?'

'I cried all the way to the airport,' she confessed, as if that should make it easier for him.

It didn't. 'Don't *ever* leave me like that again!'

'I won't,' she promised.

He sunk them into another hot deep hungry kiss that didn't last long enough before he was pulling right back. 'No, you won't,' he agreed. 'Because I am going to make sure that you don't!'

His hand went into his pocket and came out again, holding a small black leather box.

The moment Antonia saw it she knew what it was. And on a choke of dismay, she said, 'No,' and snapped her hands behind her back. 'You don't have to do that.'

She even started backing away.

He followed. 'Of course I do.' He reached for her.

'No!' she cried, and almost bounced as her shoulders hit the wall behind her.

Marco started frowning. '*Amore*, this is what *I* want. It is what we *both* want!'

But she kept on shaking her head. 'I came back,' she repeated. 'I don't need this to keep me here! A ring will just make everything more complicated! I would rather—'

'It's okay,' he said soothingly. 'I squared it with my father. He—'

Her eyes shot to his. Her mouth trembled. 'You told your father about me?' She looked so horrified it hurt. 'But you had no right to upset him with this when he's ill!'

'Ill,' Marco agreed. 'Not incompetent! And it is out of respect for his illness that I sought his approval. But do you honestly think I am the kind of man who requires the approval of anyone?'

'You require mine,' she pointed out. 'And I am not prepared to come between you and your parents. I don't *need* to do that. I am perfectly happy with things as they were.'

'Well, I'm not,' he announced, his eyes narrowing on the sudden leap of anxiety that claimed her eyes. His teeth began to glint like a tiger preparing to take his first bite. 'So I made my father an offer he couldn't refuse,' he slid in silkily—and followed her until his arm could rest against the wall near her head. 'I said it was either done this way—' he lifted the box close to her nose '—or I used less—conventional methods.'

'There aren't any.'

In reply he swooped on her mouth. She died for that kiss. Of course she did. 'An illegitimate Bellini child is just not acceptable,' he murmured as he drew away again. 'My father saw my point and—'

'You mean you threatened to make me pregnant?' she gasped. Then her expression hardened. 'Do you honestly think I would allow you to do that to me?' His eyes began to gleam with a taunting message: You haven't got the will-power to stop me.

But she had. On this point, if on no other, she had the power to say no to him. 'A child isn't a pawn, Marco,' she said, stepping sideways and away from him. 'You don't play Russian roulette with its future just to win an argument.'

'Is that the voice of experience?' His expression had turned curious. She flashed him a wary look. 'Anton Gabrielli,' he announced. 'And a cheque for a serious amount of lira. He was either paying off a mistress or buying your silence,' he explained with a shrug. 'And as I was sure you've only ever been *my* mistress, I came to the conclusion he was buying the silence. You won't believe how good I felt about it.'

He might but she didn't. She was seeing the glimmer of a chance at an old Italian name making the difference between unacceptable and acceptable. 'I won't acknowledge him as my father, you know,' she warned him. 'If he announced it to the world I would deny the charge. He will not be walking me down any church aisle just to make me respectable. And if he left me his millions, I would give them straight back again. So if this—' she flicked an expressive hand at the ring box '—honour you are now prepared to bestow on me is built on those assumptions, you're backing a losing horse here, Marco.'

'His *billions* will go to his son and heir,' he informed her levelly, and saw her flicker of surprise. 'I see you didn't know about him.' Marco smiled. 'Handsome guy. Likes the ladies. Plays the field with relish—much like his father did. Married,' he added succinctly. 'Two children—a boy and a girl. The wife lives with her father-in-law on their private estate on the island of Capri, while her husband enjoys himself elsewhere. As for the Gabrielli name, he can keep it since you will be taking the *Bellini* name. And if you don't want him as a father, then fine.' He shrugged. 'Because I have one worthy of taking on that role for you. And, despite your natural opinion of both my parents, they are really quite nice people. Their biggest problem is that they love me too much. But in time I am hoping to spread that around a bit to other, newer members of the family.'

'Your mother hates me—'

'My mother,' Marco took up. 'Was so repentant when I saw her this afternoon that she wanted to come back to the apartment to tell you so. Fortunately—' he grimaced '—I talked her out of it. Or she would have been witnessing her son's complete downfall. Interested in that?' he quizzed her softly.

Her eyes filled with guilty tears. Her mouth began to tremble. He wanted to kiss it until it was warm and red and too full of him to tremble ever again. Instead, he pocketed the ring. She watched him do it, and he was very pleased to see her eyes darken and the way she had to turn and walk away in an effort to hide her disappointment. She might make all the claims in the world about not wanting the ring, but she was lying; she wanted *it* almost as much as she wanted *him*.

But now she could wait. He had handled it badly anyway. And this was not the setting in which he preferred to commit himself to marriage. So they were leaving—now, he decided. Except first…

He spotted everything he required and went over to collect a sheet of brown paper and a roll of sticky tape. She was standing by the window, staring out on the kind of view of Milan that gave this scruffy room reason. Ignoring her, he went over to the nude portrait of himself and, with the efficiency of one who knew exactly how to handle an unframed canvas, he started to package it ready for transportation.

Glancing at him over her shoulder, she didn't even attempt to protest at what he was doing other than to say quietly, 'It isn't finished.'

'You may have all the time in the world to do so back at the apartment,' he replied. Sticky tape screeched as he stretched it over brown paper. 'We will convert one of the guest bedrooms into a studio.' Sharp white teeth neatly sliced through the tape, long fingers smoothed it into place.

'Marco—'

'Is there anything you want to take with you now, or can the rest wait until we are more able to receive it?' he cut in smoothly, then lifted the canvas down and finally looked at her.

Although the sunlight might be wearing the warm-gold of the late afternoon, the way it touched her hair and her skin reminded him of her own self-portrait. But the expression in her eyes could have been her mother's. Sad. It was sad. She didn't believe there was any hope for them.

'You came back, *cara*,' he reminded her soberly. 'But you did so to a new order of things. That order cannot be returned to what it used to be because you are afraid of what the change may mean.'

'It can if you let it,' she argued.

But he shook his dark head. '*I* no longer want what we used to have,' he explained, so succinctly that Antonia had no choice but to understand his meaning.

Her eyes grew so dark that his heart hit his ribcage. It was obvious she saw the choice he was giving her—between leaving him again or facing their future with all its complications—as equal to standing between a black hole and oblivion.

But she *had* come back, he grimly reminded himself. It was the only thing that stopped him from going over there and promising her anything so long as she agreed to stay with him.

It was a strange sensation, this fear of losing her, he noted as his eyes—and his bluff—held firm. 'Ready?' he prompted.

She lowered her eyes, turned away, ran her fingers up her arms to her shoulders as if she was trying to hug something to her. Courage? The chill of fear? The love he knew she felt for him? The need to believe that he felt the same about her?

It was time she began trusting in that word 'love', he thought grimly. Time she began to trust *him*.

'Yes, I'm ready,' she said quietly.

Relief almost floored him. He had to turn away to grimace at the way his legs had just turned to nothing.

'Let's go, then.' Still holding the painting, he went to collect her bit of luggage. As she approached he silently handed over her shoulder bag, then just as silently turned to the door.

CHAPTER ELEVEN

THE apartment had a hushed air about it after the taxi ride across the noisy city. A large flat brown card package leant against one of the walls with the Romano Gallery name printed on it. Marco went to place his new find beside it, then walked away down the hall and into their bedroom with her suitcase.

He was making some statement about ownership, Antonia recognised that as she followed him. Strange, then, that stepping into the one room where she'd always believed she truly belonged she should suddenly feel as if she was entering alien territory. Yet nothing had changed, the room looked exactly as it should do— if you didn't count the absence of her few personal possessions.

Marco was already putting the case away in the cupboard. There was a statement in the way he did that, also, because the case had not been unpacked and he was shutting the door, turning the key in the lock and even went so far as to remove the key and pocket it.

Try running off with only what you came here with, now, the action yelled at her.

Unsure how to respond, Antonia was still considering her options when he came back towards her, shut the bedroom door with one hand and removed her bag from her shoulder with the other then simply let it drop. And every action was so deliberate that he set her nerve-ends tingling. Her hand was caught next. He used it to trail her behind him over to the window where he touched the switch that sent the vertical blinds sliding across the glass.

The room became shrouded in a soft half-light. Seduction suddenly eddied in the air. Turning her towards to him, he looked down at her, searched her whole face as if he had forgotten what it looked like, then sighed a small sigh.

'Why the closed blinds?' she asked him. He had never bothered to do that before.

'Ambience,' he replied. 'A desire for your full attention,' he added. 'And the need to shut the rest of the world out while we remind each other what it was we almost lost.'

'I'm sorry,' Antonia said. 'I—'

'Don't *ever* use those words to me again,' he cut in harshly. 'Especially *not* in English.' He even shuddered. 'They will always represent to me the coldest little goodbye a man could experience.'

He was talking about her text message. Her heart found her throat and blocked it as she gazed into his pain darkened blue-grey eyes. *I'm sorry* hovered on her lips again. She converted the words into a tender-sweet kiss meant to convey the meaning for her.

Pain-dark changed to passion-dark. '*Si*,' he whispered in approval. The kiss was most definitely preferable to words for him.

So one tender kiss led to another, until tender became hungry and hunger converted itself into desire. Desire stripped clothes away in a slow precious reacquainting with what she had put at risk today.

This was it. All she needed, she told herself. This man looking at her like this, touching her like this—*needing* her like this. Anything else he cared to bestow was merely a bonus. Because she could feel the love emanating from him even though he had never said the words to her.

But, as she had just demonstrated, words weren't necessary when there were other ways to relay your feelings. It was special. What they had was special. So they made love as if this was their first time. And as one day slipped harmoniously into another, Antonia began likening it to a honeymoon, where neither was seemingly prepared to allow anything to spoil what they had together.

Who wanted a betrothal ring? Who wanted a marriage proposal? This was so much more comfortable. So much more her perception of what real love was about.

On Monday, Marco slipped back into his work routine without so much as hinting that he couldn't trust her to be there when he came home again. And Antonia began converting one of the guest bedrooms into her studio. Tuesday was the day she remembered the two paintings that had disappeared from the hallway and made a note to ask Marco where they had gone, only to forget completely when he arrived home that evening with a letter from Anton Gabrielli. It was an acknowledgement that she was indeed his daughter, apologising for his behaviour, and offering to announce her as such if she wished him to do so.

'Did you bully him into this?' she asked Marco.

'I merely made him see the error in his judgement of you,' he replied. 'I thought you deserved that. What you do about him now is, of course, your own decision.'

'So you aren't going to persuade me into making his relationship to me public?'

It was a challenge, and Marco recognised it as such. 'I don't need him, *cara*,' he stated it quietly. 'But I wondered if you might feel the need to know him better one day.'

'I won't,' she said adamantly. 'It turns me cold just to look at his name.'

'Then put the letter away,' Marco advised, 'and forget about him. He won't trouble you again, I promise you.'

Which made her wonder what influence he had brought to bear on a man like Anton Gabrielli that he could sound so sure about that. But she didn't ask, didn't want to spoil her new grasp on happiness by contaminating it with questions she really didn't want the answers to.

Wednesday, they went out to dinner with Franco and Nicola, who were just back from their visit to Lake Como. Nicola looked radiant. Her eyes shone with pleasure because it was so very obvious that Antonia and Marco had sorted out their differences. Everyone enjoyed themselves. It was just as it used to be.

Thursday and Friday she devoted to overseeing the transfer of her artist's studio to its new location, and not once... Well, maybe once or twice she found herself thinking wistfully back to a certain ring box she had last seen disappearing into Marco's pocket never to see again. But then she would pull herself together and get on with whatever it was she was doing. She was content. She was happy. Marco was making her a permanent part of his life and he loved her; she was sure of it. Or becoming more sure of it as the days went by.

Then he ruined it.

It came so unexpectedly that it just hadn't occurred to her how she had been living the last week, cocooned in her own sweet dream-world constructed around a comfortable self-denial, until, over breakfast on

Saturday, he murmured casually, 'We are going out to-night. A party. I think we will go shopping for something really special for you to wear...'

A party, she repeated. A party meant people. People meant facing her public humiliation from the week before. She couldn't do it. 'No,' she breathed.

Lifting his eyes from his ever-present morning newspaper, he narrowed them on her paling face. 'Red,' he murmured softly. 'I think we will go for something truly outrageous in red. Long. Slinky. Strapless and backless to show off your wonderful skin.'

'I'm not going, Marco,' she announced more firmly.

'Wear your hair up,' he continued as if she hadn't spoken. 'Let everyone see your beautiful neck and know that the only man allowed to put his lips to it is me...'

'I said, I'm not going!' She jerked to her feet.

'And I will drip you in diamonds.' He refused to take any notice of her. 'Ears, throat, wrists—even a sexy anklet sounds really irresistible.'

'Why don't you just hang a sign round my neck saying *Scarlet Woman*?' she flashed at him angrily.

Sitting back in his chair, he grinned at the image. 'Red-painted mouth. Lots of black mascara. And I think a red carnation in your hair might just make the whole ensemble perfect.'

He even kissed the tips of his fingers. Antonia had never felt so hurt in all her life. 'I can't believe you're talking like this to me, when you *know* what happened the last time you took me into company!'

She was pulsing with hurt, with fright, with indignation, Marco observed ruefully. But he didn't question any of those emotions. In fact he absolutely understood her right to feel them.

But as for the rest? 'Are you ashamed of who you are, *cara*?' he queried curiously.

Her chin went up. 'No,' she denied.

'Ashamed of being my woman, then?'

'I won't be pilloried a second time.'

Which was a neat way of getting out of giving him the answer to his question. He stood up. She made to spin away. He held her in place with the firm grip of his hands on her waist. Trapped by the table, their chairs, and his hands, she had no choice but to remain exactly where she was. But the tension in her body was enormous, the need to run again so palpable he could actually feel it dancing along every muscle she possessed.

'We made a deal a week ago,' he reminded her.

'Deal?' Her eyes flickered restlessly to his, then away again. 'I don't know what you're talking about.'

Liar, he thought grimly. 'You returned to me wanting the same as what you almost left behind.' He spelled it out to her anyway. 'I told you you couldn't have that.'

'But we've been so happy this week!' she cried. 'Why do you want to mess with something that's working fine!'

'This week I've played it your way. I've allowed us to hide and pretend everything is *fine* because you seemed to need to do that. But I don't want *fine* I want *perfect*,' he added. 'And perfect comes at a price, *cara*. The point is, are you prepared to pay it?'

She clearly didn't like the sound of the word. It was like holding a tiger by its tail. 'And what is this price?'

'Your trust,' he announced. 'I want you to *trust* me to make this work for us. And, just so you understand how serious I am, I must warn you that I will accept nothing less than your total trust.'

Nothing less—as in *nothing*. No Marco at all was what he was saying here. Antonia shivered at the mere prospect. 'And this trust comes in the colour red.' Her sigh turned itself into a grimace.

'In your face, knock them dead red,' he confirmed. 'Will you do it?'

Trust him not to hold her up as an object of scorn? No, she didn't. For you didn't dress your woman up, as he had just described, without having some ulterior motive for doing it. But to demand to know what that motive was had now been denied her by that word *trust*.

So, 'Yes,' she said.

His soft laugh said he was aware of how difficult she'd found it to say that word. But, 'Good,' was all he replied. 'Because I've seen the perfect dress on Via Monte Napoleon. Let's go and buy it...'

It was certainly red, Antonia confirmed, as she stood looking at herself in the bedroom mirror. In your face *and* knock them dead. A quiver of anxiety went shivering through her. In fact, Marco had described it perfectly. Long and slinky, with a heart-shaped boned bodice that defied gravity and a back that wasn't there at all. Pinched-in waistline, a long skirt that clung smoothly to every detail of her shape as it made its way down to her ankles, and a kick-back pleat that began at the back of her knees to give her the ability to walk— and her figure an hourglass shape that was so damn sexy it couldn't be more 'in your face'.

Her hair was up, as requested, and she truly did drip with diamonds. Diamond choker, diamond bracelet at her wrist, diamonds dangling from her ears. Glancing down at her high-heeled strappy red shoes, she caught a glimpse of the diamond anklet he had insisted she wear. In fact the only thing she had been able to refuse, and get away with it, was the red carnation to dress up her hair.

Her lipstick was red, her eyeliner so much more pronounced than she would usually wear it that, as she looked into her own eyes, she didn't recognise them. She looked lush, she looked sexy, and she looked like a wealthy man's possession.

Which she was, she acknowledged.

And if this wasn't dressing up to brazen out whatever was coming, then she didn't know what was.

'If I come near, will you attack me?' a deep voice quizzed her.

Her eyes flashed to him via the mirror. Big and lean, too darn handsome for his own good in conventional black dinner suit and bow-tie, he was looking at her as if he wanted to eat her alive as she stood there.

'I wonder how many propositions I will get tonight?' she mused by way of getting a hit back at him without the suggested physical attack.

Stepping behind her, he slid his hands around her narrow waist, his thumb-pads gently stroking against her bare skin. She quivered in response, despite not wanting to. The sensation centred itself deep in her abdomen and refused to budge.

Sex, it was called. Give it to me. He saw it reflected in her eyes. 'They can try, *mi amante*, but we both know to whom it is that you belong, hmm?'

Yes, she thought, and for a moment actually hated him for being so sure of himself. It could not go unchallenged, though. So she turned in his grasp and stroked a hand up his dress shirt, found his warm throat, trailed her fingers up to his ear. This man might know her inside out, but she knew him also. The pleasure point behind his ear only needed the lightest of caress to send a shudder through him.

'And you know to whom it is that *you* belong, hey, *mi amore*?'

He caught the trailing fingers, kissed them with a wryly mocking bow, his eyes dark with promises as he straightened again. It was only then that she saw the colour of his jacket lining. It was glossy silk, matador-red.

He was most definitely out to make a very big statement tonight, she realised. 'Where are we going?' She frowned up at him.

'So you thought to ask at last,' he smiled. 'Well, wait and see. It's a surprise.'

Opening her red-painted mouth to tell him that she didn't like surprises, she felt the dark eyes challenge her. She held her breath, thought about that wretched word *trust*, and closed her mouth again.

He rewarded her with a kiss that required his mouth to be wiped clear of lipstick later and her to do a quick refurbishing job on her own.

After that they left the apartment and went downstairs to climb into the back of a chauffeur-driven limousine, which meant that Marco intended to enjoy a drink tonight. It wasn't late, which was unusual here in Milan, where most parties tended to begin way after ten. But she didn't begin to understand why they had set out so early until they arrived at Linate airport, to a waiting helicopter.

'Tell me where we are going,' she pleaded, unable to stop herself.

Helping her into the rear of the helicopter, and making sure her dress was neatly folded around her ankles as she sat down, he joined her, closed the door, gave the pilot the nod to get them into the air, then turned and announced very casually, 'We are going to my parents' home in Tuscany...'

Nothing—nothing had prepared her for that announcement. Marco could see that as her face went perfectly white. She didn't speak, didn't even gasp in shocked horror; she just sat beside him and died a thousands deaths in total silence.

His instincts were telling him to say something—anything to reassure her that this night was going to be fine. But that word *fine* wasn't enough for him. And the word *trust* was demanding he make her give him that unequivocally. It was a pride thing; he knew that. For, although he might have forgiven her for keeping so much of herself hidden from him, he still hadn't come to terms with how little she had trusted him with any of the important issues in her life.

Shallow. She'd thought him shallow. An arrogant snob who was quite capable of loving a woman senseless in his bed but could actually despise her for what she was. Well, tonight, she was going to learn a few harsh lessons. And one of them was to spend the next hour stewing in her own anxieties. He felt she owed him that.

And anyway, he was excited. He was out to make an impact tonight, and not just on his family and friends but on Antonia too. So, with the smoothness taught to him from the cradle, he began talking, filling in the trip with innocuous discussion about innocuous subjects that forced her to think and answer but did not detract from the tense expectancy that built up the longer they were in the air.

They arrived as darkness was falling. It was the perfect time to get her first glimpse of the Casa Bellini.

The vine-covered valley, the house in its centre lit from the inside by electric lighting while the final drape of the sun coloured a blush against its outer walls.

Waiting for the helicopter blades to go still before he jumped out, Marco turned to lift Antonia down. She slid through his grasp like smooth bone china, no weight, no substance, nothing but fairness and beauty and an anxiety that kicked at his gut.

'I love you,' he murmured, and placed a kiss on her brow.

It was the first time he had said it out loud. Impact was what he had been out for; impact was what he got. Her eyes washed with moisture, and he felt his own want to do the same.

'I just wanted to be sure you knew that before we went inside,' he added very huskily—so huskily, in fact, that he didn't know his own voice.

She didn't say anything. He didn't think she could. So he took her hand and walked her towards his parents' house and in through the huge French windows left open to the evening air. Her fingers clung so tightly to his he knew—*knew* this woman, this beautiful woman was his for ever now.

The first people they saw as they entered were his mother and father, waiting to greet them on the huge expanse of brown and white chequered floor that gave their home such a grand entrance that led right from the front to the back of the house.

This was it, he thought. Show time…

Dressed in statutory black, but breathtakingly elegant in it, Signora Isabella Bellini walked forwards. She was smiling at her, Antonia noticed. It was an uncertain, slightly wary smile, but at least it was a smile. She tried a smile in return.

'Welcome,' Marco's mother greeted, and leaned forward to place a kiss on each of her cheeks.

Her fingers tightened their grip on Marco.

'Th-thank you.' Antonia wasn't sure why she offered those words in English. It simply seemed appropriate. 'It was good of you to invite me here.'

'No.' Signora Bellini did not accept that. 'It should have happened a long time ago. I apologise for my rudeness and hope you can learn to forgive me for it. We Bellinis can be too arrogant for our own comfort sometimes.'

It was so gracious, so kind, Antonia felt the tears threaten again. 'I understood, really I did,' she assured the older woman. Well—maybe it was a lie, but it was a *kind* lie.

It was a good point for Federico Bellini to step smoothly into the breach. 'Now I see why my son lays threats at a sick man's door,' he remarked, softening the censure with a lazy grin which hit Antonia right in her solar plexus because it was so like Marco's smile.

He was tall like his son, dark-haired like his son—if a little peppered with silver. But it was also clear that, beneath the sophistication of formal black and white clothing, the rest of Signor Bellini had seen better times.

Opening her mouth to voice her concern for his illness, the man himself pre-empted her by bending towards her. 'Don't say it,' he confided. 'It is not necessary.' Then he kissed both her cheeks, raised his head and smiled his son's smile again. 'It's an honour to meet you at last, Miss Carson.'

Then he turned his attention to Marco. 'This is your

night, Marco. Your guests await. Therefore I suggest you get this started.'

With that hand still firmly clasped in his, Marco felt Antonia's instant tension, the shock in realising that this was more than just a formal introduction to his parents.

His father's eyes were glinting with sardonic knowledge. His mother was displaying no expression at all. She had not been against what he had set up here, but she had not been sure it was the right way to go about settling the issue of Antonia.

'Hurt her with this and she will never forgive you,' she'd warned him only yesterday.

'You don't know her as I do,' he'd replied. 'I have confidence in her. I *trust* her to understand.'

Trust. *Dio,* but that word was playing a major role in his life right now, he acknowledged as he started walking towards the doors which led into the family's formal reception room.

Antonia clung to his side. His parents fell into step behind them. As they reached the doors a waiting servant smoothly pushed them open to reveal a vast room lit by huge mountains of crystal. Marco paused on the threshold, so he could give Antonia a moment to absorb the sheer grandeur of the room and the people who were already present and waiting for their entrance.

The hum of conversation dropped into silence. Faces turned, people stared. Beside him, Antonia's pulse began to quicken as she took in the full impact of the whole assembly. And Marco did nothing, just waited for her restless eyes to finish making a full inventory of what he had set up for them here tonight.

Then at last she saw them, standing out like a pair of statements. Bold, brash, utterly scorning any hint of discomfort. Her warm soft red-painted mouth slackened, her ensuing gasp audible only to him. Surprise tingled from her fingers into his, then she simply stood there so breathless and still that he actually began to wonder if he had made a big mistake.

This just wasn't happening, Antonia tried to tell herself. She was having a dream. A very weird dream. She had to be. In a minute all of these people were going to start laughing in gruesome mockery, telling her to get out and never come near them again, which was how dreams like these usually finished. It was the only answer she could form to what it was she was looking at.

But it wasn't a dream. She knew it because she could feel Marco literally vibrating with waiting tension beside her. She tried swallowing and found she couldn't. She tried turning to look at him, but she couldn't do that either because her eyes were refusing to move from what they had frozen on.

For right there, hanging on his parents' wall for everyone to see, were two nudes painted in oils and mounted in matching frames. One was herself, looking slender and sleek and coyly seductive. The other was Marco, looking as bold and arrogant in his nakedness as she'd always perceived him to be.

Heat roared into her cheeks, then faded away again. Her heart began to thunder on the total shock of seeing the two of them so brazenly presented like this. And suddenly the dress began to make sense, the desire to drip her in diamonds. Marco was taking them all on— his parents, his friends, all those mocking doubters who didn't believe he could love this woman who could expose her body like this.

If you can't beat them, join them, he was saying. If I can't make them believe, then—what the heck? Throw these two paintings in their faces and let them think what they like!

'If you can hack it then I can too,' Marco murmured beside her, and his voice was soft, layered with warmth and humour and a lazy challenge.

She found the strength to look at him, saw the humour reflecting in his eyes, plus something else—a plea, maybe, for her to understand what it was he had been trying to achieve when he'd decided to do this.

A short laugh rippled from her. It spilled into her eyes and turned his smile into a grin. She looked frontward again—and continued to smile, because she understood. She *knew*! This was his way of levelling the differences in them. It was *him* coming down his lofty ladder. It was *her* climbing up to meet him.

The hand he placed on her lower spine threaded electric sensation across her naked skin as it began drifting up her spine to her slender nape in an act of sensual possession.

'More to come,' he warned softly, and urged her into movement again.

Her legs felt like rubber. Her pulse was racing, and her mind was lost in a haze of shock and some dismay and a whole lot of sinfully delicious elation. He took them past smiling faces, past rueful faces, past familiar faces like Franco and Nicola. She saw, through what felt like a misted glaze, Stefan grinning knowingly at her, while the woman at his side looked on curiously. She was tall and dark and so beautiful it made Antonia halt for a second to offer her a warm smile.

'Tanya.' She whispered the woman's name.

'Later,' Marco advised, and pressed her into movement again.

At the other end of the room, he finally paused. It

was a staged arrival, which placed them exactly in between their naked images. Lights sparkled, diamonds
flashed, faces observed curiously as he turned her towards him.

Holding the whole room captive, he looked deep into
her eyes, then dropped his gaze to her mouth and allowed it to linger there until the pulse of anticipation
became an energy charge all of its own.

'Right,' he said huskily, 'now, this is the deal...'

'Another one?' she whispered back, aware that he
was deliberately holding her balanced on a pin-head of
expectation with the warmth of his eyes and the promise
of his kiss, and the touch of his fingers on her—

She glanced down and had to blink several times before she could focus on the ring he was carefully sliding
onto her finger. Made of gold and platinum, it was an
intricate twist of finely worked metals forming the clasp
for a diamond. And not just any old diamond, she realised, as she watched its flawless quality sparkle with a
deep yellow lustre which told her instinctively that this
was a very rare diamond indeed.

'What do you think?' Deep, dark, disturbingly husky,
his voice made her senses sparkle like the diamond.

'It's—beautiful,' she breathed.

'At the risk of sounding really corny, it reminded me
of your eyes,' he drily confessed. 'But it comes with a
price-tag attached to it,' he then added.

'Another one of those also?' she murmured in an attempt to mock. But it didn't come off, for she was just
too filled with the wonder in what he was creating for
her.

It was pure romance tied up in bows of spicy sensation. The kind of thing you remembered for ever and
relayed to your children and your grandchildren.

'Mmm,' he murmured, and it was one of the really sexy murmurs that she loved so much. 'Because with this ring, *mi amore*, I am about to commit you to a solemn promise that you will trust me to love you for the rest of your life…'

It was too much. Without a care for who was watching, she reached up on tiptoe and kissed him. Not shy and light, or tender and sweet, but with every ounce of love she had in her.

A camera bulb flashed. They were caught for posterity locked in a heated embrace with two oil paintings framing why they were kissing like that…

The villa in Portofino was the ideal setting for their honeymoon, Marco thought with a sense of warm satisfaction. They'd flown in by helicopter direct from their wedding reception at his family estate in Tuscany. And though it was dark outside the air was fresher here, so close to the ocean, so Marco had no problem leaning against the balcony rail while he watched his bride come towards him.

She was naked, of course. But then so was he—if you didn't count the rich cream-satin waistcoat she had made him put back on before she would allow him to make love to her. It was meant to make a statement, like the fine tulle veil she still had pinned to her beautiful hair, that floated around her exquisite face and shoulders as she moved towards him.

Sexy. Very sexy. He allowed himself a lecherous grin. 'When are you going to take it off?' he asked lazily.

'When I feel married,' she replied.

He arched a brow. 'And you don't feel married yet?'

'No.' The pout was very spoiled and sumptuously

kissable. And, since they'd already made love several
times since they'd arrived here, it was also a slight on
his virility.

'Watch it,' he warned.

She had the audacity to look down. He laughed—
what else could he do when he was being bewitched by
a teasing little temptress with only one thing on her
mind.

Dio, she made him feel good. She made him feel like
the only worthy man on this earth.

Her fingers came out, stroked the cream satin lapel
up to his shoulders, then made their way back down
again. When she reached the open buttons she began to
slowly close them. The cutaway edges of the waistcoat
suddenly put a whole new meaning on erotic fantasy.

'If you're looking so intent because you're thinking
of painting me like this, then take my advice, *cara*, and
change your mind,' he advised.

Lightly said, lazily delivered, but still he meant every
word of it. Her chin came up. The pout had gone; the
seductress had switched back on. Stepping that tiny bit
closer to him, she held his eyes for a long moment and
caught his mouth with a kiss aimed to take the legs from
under him—while her hands went in search of other
weaknesses.

His eyes drew shut, his breath escaped on a thickened
sigh as she unleashed her magic upon him. If he died
right now, at least he would go taking this image with
him.

Man and wife, belonging to each other.

'You have no inhibition,' he censured darkly.

'I love you,' she answered simply. 'It *is* uninhibited.'

She was right, and it was. The warm, red, kiss-
swollen mouth he claimed with his own mouth. The
woman he claimed in other ways.

Modern Romance™
...seduction and
passion guaranteed

Tender Romance™
...love affairs that
last a lifetime

Sensual Romance™
...sassy, sexy and
seductive

Blaze™
...sultry days and
steamy nights

Medical Romance™
...medical drama on
the pulse

Historical Romance™
...rich, vivid and
passionate

29 new titles every month.

*With all kinds of Romance for
every kind of mood...*

MILLS & BOON®

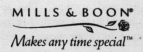

Makes any time special™

MAT4

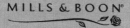

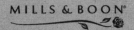